The Great
Googlestein Museum
Mystery

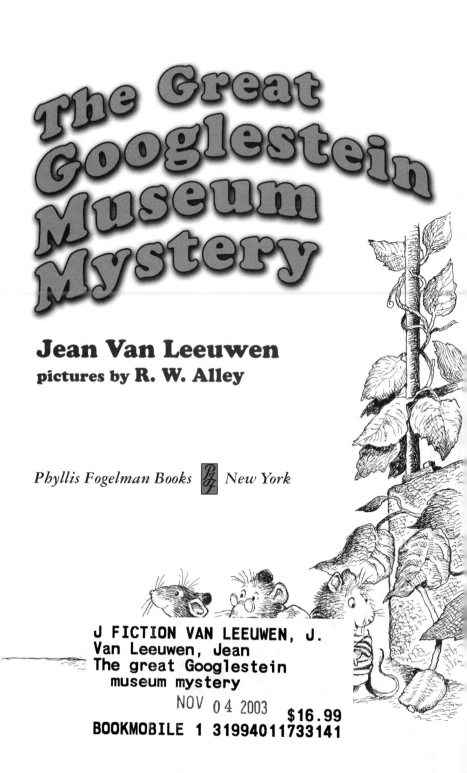

The Great Googlestein Museum Mystery

Jean Van Leeuwen
pictures by **R. W. Alley**

Phyllis Fogelman Books *New York*

Published by Phyllis Fogelman Books
An imprint of Penguin Putnam
Books for Young Readers
345 Hudson Street
New York, New York 10014
Text copyright © 2003 by Jean Van Leeuwen
Pictures copyright © 2003 by R. W. Alley
Designed by Jasmin Rubero
Text set in Garamond 3
Printed in the U.S.A. on acid-free paper

10 9 8 7 6 5 4 3 2 1

Library of Congress Cataloging-in-Publication Data
Van Leeuwen, Jean.
The great Googlestein Museum mystery /
by Jean Van Leeuwen ; pictures by R. W. Alley.
p.   cm.
Summary: Three adventurous mice escape from
their home in Macy's department store and spend
an exciting week in the Guggenheim Museum,
creating a sensation in the art world.
ISBN 0-8037-2765-8
[1. Mice—Fiction. 2. Solomon R. Guggenheim Museum—
Fiction. 3. Art—Fiction. 4. New York (N.Y.)—Fiction.]
I. Alley, R. W. (Robert W.), ill. II. Title.
PZ7.V3273 Grf 2003
[Fic]—dc21   2001051273

Table of Contents

The Great
Googlestein Museum
Mystery

1

I Decide to
Go Outside

"I never saw so many rabbits in my whole life," says Fats.

Looking out the window of our little house, I have to agree. All around us, as far as I can see, are nothing but rabbits. Large ones and little ones. Fat ones and skinny ones. Fluffy ones and flat ones. Pink ones and white ones. Even a giant rabbit as tall as a human. This is like a bad dream.

I blink, then look again. That giant rabbit is still there. Maybe I've fallen down a rabbit hole.

A rabbit hole filled with baskets. The giant rabbit is holding one, and so are some of the smaller ones. Looking around, I see nearly as many baskets as rabbits.

"Do you smell it?" Fats asks suddenly. His nose is pointed in the air, sniffing. "Could it be?" Now his whiskers start to quiver. "Yes, I'm sure of it." A big grin spreads across his face. "Jelly beans!"

Rabbits, baskets, jelly beans. What is going on here?

"Oh, boy, jelly beans!" Fats is bouncing up and down with excitement. He is always this way when he smells food. Any minute now I may have to grab him by the tail so he doesn't fall out the window.

All this commotion brings Raymond from his easy chair, where he has been working on his daily crossword puzzle, to join us.

"Oh, my," he says, peering outside. "Look at those Easter rabbits."

Of course. I haven't fallen down a rabbit hole after all. Those are Easter rabbits.

What exactly are Easter rabbits? I wonder. But I don't ask. After all, I, Merciless Marvin the Magnificent, am the leader of this gang. Leaders are supposed to know everything.

Luckily Fats asks the question. "What's an Easter rabbit?"

Raymond, naturally, knows all about them. He reads a lot. In fact, he reads anything he can get his paws on: bubble gum wrappers, sales slips, newspapers, magazines, books. One winter he even read his way through an entire set of encyclopedias.

"It is the strange custom of humans," Raymond explains, "to celebrate the holiday of Easter by giving toy rabbits to children. Also, I believe, toy ducks and chickens. And baskets filled with candy eggs. I don't understand it, but it appears to be some kind of celebration of spring."

This is strange, all right. Something like the way humans celebrate the holiday of Christmas with that fat guy in the red suit and the reindeer with a lightbulb for a nose. But I don't dwell on the strangeness of humans, with which I am quite familiar. For I have just heard Raymond utter the magic word. Spring!

Finally. It has been a long, dreary winter in the toy department of Macy's department store, where I live with my gang in our own little dollhouse hidden away on a top shelf. We have played with all the toys, from electric trains and racing cars (my personal favorites) to chess sets (Raymond's) to silly board games like Candyland (Fats's all-time top choice). We have raided the gourmet shop a hundred times. We have watched so many old gangster movies in the TV department that I know all the tough-guy lines by heart. And Raymond has moved on from encyclopedias to computer manuals.

Raymond is not bored. After studying all those manuals, he is thinking of building his own computer. And Fats is happy as long as the gourmet shop is well-stocked with cheese, pickles, and chocolate chip cookies. But I am a mouse who loves adventure. I hate being cooped up inside, even in the comfortable surroundings of our dollhouse home.

That is when I decide.

"Gang," I say in my best leader voice. "We are going to get away from these rabbits and baskets and jelly beans. We're going Outside to take a look at spring. Today."

"But, Marvin," protests Raymond right away. "It is broad daylight. Look at the hundreds of shoppers out there. Look at all those sharp heels and stroller wheels."

Raymond tends to be the nervous type. After all my years of training, even after giving him his name, Raymond the Rat, to make him think tough, he still remains a worrier.

I take another look out the window. I hate to admit it, but Raymond has a point. The toy department is crowded with shoppers: mothers and fathers, old ladies, little kids, babies in strollers. For a mouse, sharp heels and stroller wheels are to be avoided whenever possible.

"I don't want to get away from jelly beans," puts in Fats. "I want to get *to* them."

Food, food. That is Fats's life.

"We will wait until closing time," I tell Raymond. "And we'll pick up some jelly beans along the way," I tell Fats.

That is all it takes to make my gang agree.

It is hard for me to wait. My tail is twitching and my toes are tapping, I am so eager for the fun to begin. But I watch out the window until, finally, the crowd begins to thin out. It is almost closing time. Most of the heavy strollers have left. The sharp heels are few and far between.

"Let's go," I tell my gang. And without waiting for Raymond to object, I slip out the door.

We live on the highest shelf, with a view of the entire toy department. So I have a perfect observation post. It doesn't take me long to spot what I am looking for. A shopping bag.

I have traveled by many methods, but my favorite for covering long distances is the shopping bag. Someone else does all the work while I ride in style. Of course, there are some hazards involved. You can never be sure where your shopping bag is going. And when you reach your destination, making your escape can be tricky. I have also found that the shopping bag must be chosen with great care. Avoid shopping bags filled with hard objects like baseballs and building blocks, or sharp objects like Pick-Up Sticks. And especially beware of little old ladies who might be carrying knitting needles. I learned that lesson the hard way. The ideal shopping bag is one filled with soft pillows. Or maybe donuts.

This must be my lucky day, because I spot my target immediately. A little old lady, true. But this one is standing next to the stuffed animal counter, her arms full of rabbits. She must be buying one for each of her grandchildren. And she is sure to carry them home in a shopping bag.

"Follow me, gang," I hiss.

I am down off our shelf in a flash. Past the doll furniture, past the dolls of all shapes and sizes, past the doll carriages. Then I am darting along the floor past the games and puzzles toward the stuffed animal counter.

I glance over my shoulder to make sure my gang is with me.

They aren't.

Another quick glance tells me why. Under the games and puzzles counter Fats has found a jelly bean.

I backtrack. "What is going on?" I demand.

Fats doesn't answer. His mouth is full of jelly bean, I see.

"You promised him jelly beans," Raymond reminds me.

"Okay, Fats," I say. "You have your jelly bean. Now get moving."

And I'm off again.

This time I keep a sharp eye out to make sure my gang is following me. Raymond is right behind me. And behind him I can hear Fats puffing and panting, trying to keep up. Until I reach the music counter.

No puffing. No panting. No Fats.

Once again I have to backtrack. I find Fats sitting beside a parked stroller, taking a lick of a pink jelly bean while in his other paw he holds a

yellow one. As I watch, a purple one falls from the sky.

"Fats!" I give him my most severe glare. "We're going to miss our ride."

"I can't help it, Marvin," he answers. "It's raining jelly beans."

I look up. A little kid with a sticky face and a big smile is sitting in this stroller, holding a bag of jelly beans. He eats one, then drops one on the floor. Eats another, drops one on the floor.

This is great for Fats, who is in jelly bean heaven. But not so great for my plan to go Outside.

I can see this calls for extreme measures.

"Raymond," I order. "You take his front paws. I'll take the back."

We drag Fats, kicking and grumbling, away from his great jelly bean bonanza.

I'm afraid we may be too late. By now my little old lady is probably out the door with her bag full of rabbits. By now she could even be home having a cup of tea.

But no. This must really be my lucky day. I see that the salesclerk, Mrs. Feldman, has just handed her a large shopping bag. The little old lady sets it down next to her feet for a moment, while she puts away her change. This is our opportunity.

I am taking no chances. I grab Fats firmly by the ear. Then up the side of that shopping bag we scurry. We swing over the edge, and drop down inside. As we fall, I have a brief moment of panic. What if the old lady changed her mind and didn't buy those rabbits after all? What if we find ourselves in a bag full of baseballs, building blocks, and Pick-Up Sticks?

But we make a perfect landing, through a layer of tissue paper and right into the laps of all those rabbits. They are soft as pillows, fluffy and cuddly and warm. The old lady's grandchildren are going to love them.

So does Fats.

"Oh!" he squeaks. "It's just like a featherbed."

Naturally Fats is an expert on beds as well as food.

This is the way to travel, all right. As the shopping bag begins to move, we bounce a little. Up and down, up and down. This is fun. I bounce higher. And higher.

I'm having such a good time that I don't notice it at first. But then I become aware that each time I bounce, I feel something sticky. On my nose, on my tail, in my whiskers.

Fats. It has to be.

"Fats!" I grab for his ear again. "Are you eating something?"

"Just my last jelly bean," he whimpers. "I had to finish it. It's grape."

I am tempted to give his tail a little sample of the torture twist that I perfected after watching a hundred prison movies, just to show him who's boss. But then I feel our bag being set down.

Where are we? I haven't been paying attention to our progress.

I hear a loud clunking, whining sound. I'm familiar with that one. It is a revolving door, a mouse's worst nightmare when traveling on his own.

A second later, I hear something much better. The tooting of horns, the rush of passing traffic, a far-off siren. And I smell it. Cool, refreshing, sooty city air.

This *is* my lucky day. We are Outside.

2

I Find Myself in a Strange New Place

As soon as I smell that Outside air, I am alert and ready for anything. To settle down for a nice soft ride or make a flying leap out of this shopping bag. It all depends on where our little old lady is going.

We aren't going anywhere fast, I notice. In fact, we aren't moving at all.

I pinch Fats's tail to make sure he is alert and ready.

"Ouch!" he squeals.

I am forced to sit on him.

Just at that moment I hear the word I've been

waiting forever to hear. The word I thought I never would hear.

"Taxi!" calls the little old lady.

I can't believe my ears. This is my luckiest of all lucky days. To ride in a taxi has been my life-long dream.

"We better jump out," Raymond whispers.

"Are you kidding?" I whisper back.

"But we don't know where she is going," Raymond reminds me. "We might end up in Brooklyn. Or Queens. Or even New Jersey. We might never find our way back."

I ignore his gloom and doom. I don't care where we end up. I will deal with that later. It is riding in a real taxi that matters.

A moment later I hear the screech of brakes. Then the sound of a car door opening. The shopping bag is lifted up and set down again. On the seat of a real taxi.

"Where to?" the driver asks.

"Fifth Avenue and Eighty-fifth Street," says the little old lady.

Fifth Avenue and Eighty-fifth Street. That is not Brooklyn or Queens or New Jersey. Fifth Avenue is a place we have been to before. Fats lived there for a while in a fancy apartment with a little girl named Emily, until Raymond and I rescued him and brought him back to Macy's.

"See?" I whisper to Raymond.

Then I lean back and enjoy the ride.

This is the life, all right. I could get used to this. No more sneaking around. No more dodging and weaving and hiding, always just a whisker away from annihilation. No more annoying encounters with rats, cats, and evil exterminators. "Where to?" my taxi driver would ask. And I would answer, "I believe I'll take in the circus today. Oh, and you can let Raymond off at the Public Library. And Fats at The Cheese Emporium."

Actually, now that I think of it, maybe riding in a taxi is not the ultimate luxury after all. A limousine would be even better.

While I am fantasizing about where my personal chauffeur would take me, our taxi is dodging and weaving through the city streets. This driver is fast, as fast as I am when I'm test-driving the new racing cars in the toy department. We are jounced around on our rabbits. And then, before I know it, brakes are screeching again and we come to a stop.

"How much do I owe you?" the old lady asks.

Our taxi ride is over. I waited for it all my life, and it seems like it only lasted ten seconds.

But I don't have time to think about that now. I have to prepare for our exit from this shopping bag. Already the bag is in motion.

"Be ready, gang," I warn. "When I say 'Now!'—jump!"

We climb up to the top rabbit. Taking a position behind its ear, I'm able to survey our surroundings. I have seen this Fifth Avenue scene before. The big apartment building that resembles the one Emily lived in. The green awning. The doorman in a fancy uniform guarding the door. This must be where the old lady lives.

I'm sure of one thing. We don't want to be trapped inside a Fifth Avenue apartment building again.

"Now!" I say. And I leap out of the bag.

I hit the sidewalk running. In seconds I have scrambled under a round bush next to the front door.

Seconds later, Raymond darts in beside me.

We wait for Fats. More seconds go by. No Fats.

"Where is he?" I grumble.

A lot of seconds go by.

"Come on, Fats," whispers Raymond.

Finally I stick my nose out. I see the Macy's bag. It is moving toward the door. The doorman opens the door. Oh, no! If Fats goes inside, we are in big trouble.

The little old lady pauses to talk to the doorman. At that moment, something drops from the top of the bag and rolls toward us. It looks like a wad of tissue paper. But it doesn't sound like one.

"Marvin! Raymond!" it squeals.

We reach out and grab the object and drag it under the bush.

"Fats!" I say, as he unwraps himself. "It's about time."

"What happened?" asks Raymond.

"I fell down," Fats explains, "and got stuck under all those rabbits. By the time I climbed up again, you were gone. So I decided to use a disguise." He looks extremely proud of himself. "Wasn't that good thinking?"

Raymond is a master of disguise. "Excellent thinking," he tells Fats.

"Not bad," I have to admit. Maybe all my years of training, trying to mold Fats—a mouse with an overdeveloped stomach and underdeveloped brain—into a tough guy like me, are starting to pay off.

As soon as Fats pulls himself together, I am ready for my next adventure. I know just what that adventure is going to be. I saw it from across the street when I peeked out of our shopping bag. And I remember it from our last visit to Fifth Avenue. Central Park!

Right in the middle of New York City is a bunch of greenery. Kind of like a chunk of country plunked down next to all the skyscrapers. When we were last here, I had a fine time in the park. I even took the ride of my life, soaring high above the city on a kite. I can't wait to see what other excitement we can find in Central Park.

"Oh, goody!" says Fats when I tell him. "I love Central Park." He is remembering his days with Emily, no doubt.

Of course, we have to get there first. We have to cross a wide street filled with giant buses and fast-moving taxis. But for a great leader like me, this is child's play.

"We will need—" begins Raymond.

"A disguise," I finish for him.

"We already have one," Fats puts in, wrapping

himself up again in tissue paper. "See? It's big enough for three."

So I make the decision to become garbage, Raymond's favorite all-purpose disguise. Our wad of tissue paper drifts along the edge of the sidewalk until we reach the corner. We join a cluster of people waiting for the traffic light to change. I am the lookout, making sure we keep our distance from dangerous objects like sharp heels, stroller wheels, and sniffing dogs.

Buses and taxis come grinding to a stop. The light turns green.

"Go!" I say.

Swiftly we dart across Fifth Avenue, just a little piece of trash blown by the wind. And a moment later we have a new hiding place, inside a low hedge in Central Park.

"We made it!" wheezes Fats.

"Of course," I say. I am not even winded.

We remove our disguise, which Raymond folds up for future use. Then cautiously we peek out from under our hedge.

Central Park is as busy as I remember it. Feet of all sizes, dressed in all kinds of footwear—sneakers, sandals, boots, high heels, little old lady shoes, baby shoes—walk by on the path next to us. And wheels of all sizes. Stroller wheels, of course. And baby carriage wheels and bicycle wheels and scooter wheels. And some tiny wheels. They flash by so fast, I can't be sure, but they seem to be attached to the bottom of someone's shoes. What are those?

Anything that moves that fast gets my attention. I keep watching until another set of tiny wheels appears.

I nudge Raymond. "What's that?" I ask.

"Rollerblades," he answers.

Now I remember. I have seen strange wheeled shoes like these before on the streets of New York. People who wear them appear to have magic feet. They glide along, hardly seeming to move, yet they are traveling as fast as any bicycler. It's kind of like ice-skating without the ice.

I've got to see more of these Rollerblades.

"Come on, gang," I order. And I'm out from under our hedge, following the tiny wheels.

Through tall grass, then from bush to tree trunk we go. But fast as I am, I can't quite keep up with that Rollerblader. I pause to catch my breath. Then I spot another set of tiny wheels, and we're off again. The path we are following takes a turn and suddenly, right next to it, is a road. Not a normal road with buses and taxis. This one is more like a race track.

It is filled with people going fast. Some are on bicycles. Some are on Rollerblades, racing each other. Some are on their own feet, running. I see fathers and mothers with children in little seats on the back of their bikes, and mothers jogging while pushing strollers. I even see a man with a dog in his bike basket. That dog is smiling like it's having a great time. So are the people. Of course. There is nothing better than traveling at high speed.

I decide right then and there. Somehow or other, somewhere, I am going to try this Rollerblading thing.

We watch for a long time, hidden under a tree root. I could stay there forever, but after a while my gang begins to get restless.

"I'm hungry," complains Fats.

"It's time to go home," says Raymond.

The crowd on the race track is thinning out. Reluctantly I agree.

We make our way to Fifth Avenue. Remembering our soft ride earlier, I'm in no mood for a bus or subway.

"I'll just hail us a taxi," I tell my gang.

Surprisingly, Raymond doesn't give me his shocked look. He is too busy staring at something across the street.

"Remarkable," he murmurs. "Quite fantastic. I don't think I've ever seen anything like it."

I never have either. What Raymond is looking at is a huge white building. There is nothing remarkable about that in New York City. Only

this one isn't tall and thin like a regular sky-scraper. Instead, it is short and fat. And it has the strangest shape: round and kind of curled up like a giant snail shell. It is the most peculiar-looking building I've ever seen.

"Beautiful," Raymond sighs.

"Weird," I say.

"I'm really hungry," Fats grumbles.

Raymond is muttering to himself. "I've got to see what it is. I've got to."

I am curious myself. So we wrap ourselves in our tissue paper disguise and once more cross Fifth Avenue.

Up close, the building just seems big. It is crowded with people, a few going in, a lot coming out. I see two doors, revolving and regular. Naturally, I choose regular. We wait patiently until there is a break in traffic, then make our move. In we drift.

Right away I spot a good hiding place, under a curved wood counter near the door. We remove our disguise. Now, finally, we can get a good look at the inside of this mystery building.

It is as crazy-looking on the inside as it was on the outside. Maybe even crazier. It has that same round shape, but it feels tall too. We gaze up at the ceiling, which rises about a zillion feet in the air. It seems to be made of glass and has a strange flower shape. Leading up to it is one long curling ramp that goes in a gradual spiral all the way up to the ceiling. Like a snail shell, I think again. That isn't all, though. Hung on the wall every few feet along the ramp are large, bright-colored paintings.

"Ah," says Raymond. "Now I understand. It's a museum."

A museum. I've never been inside one before, but I know what it is. That's where they put a bunch of old things no one wants anymore so people can stand around looking at them. There isn't much action in a museum, I have a feeling. It could get boring pretty fast.

"An art museum," adds Raymond, as if that makes it special.

"Art, shmart!" I scoff. That's even more boring than a regular museum. Just a lot of old pictures no one wants anymore. "Okay, gang. We saw it. We can go now."

"So soon?" protests Raymond. "We didn't even look at the pictures."

I don't waste time arguing, just slip into our disguise again. As we edge out from our hiding place, though, I notice something strange.

All the people are gone.

Not only that, but the lights have gone out. The whole place is quiet. While we were gazing at the ceiling, the museum has closed its doors.

Closed and locked its doors, we discover a moment later.

We are trapped in an art museum. This is even worse than being trapped in a Fifth Avenue apartment.

"What are we going to do?" whines Fats. "I'm really really hungry."

"Don't worry," I reassure him. "I'll think of something."

As leader of this gang, it's up to me to come up with an escape plan. I wrack my brain, trying to remember what heroes do in movies when they're locked in a museum. I can't recall seeing a movie about a museum lately. But I've seen a lot of old prison movies. What they do in prison movies is dig their way out.

"I've got it!" I announce. "We'll dig."

My gang stares at me, stunned, no doubt, by the brilliance of my idea.

"Uh, Marvin," says Raymond after a moment. "What kind of tools will we use? This floor appears to be quite hard."

I examine the floor. It is made of some kind of stone. "Hmmm." I pace up and down, wracking my brain some more. There has to be a way around this little problem.

"I know," says Fats. "We'll blast!" He is especially fond of the parts in movies where things are blown up. That is how he got his nickname Fats the Fuse.

Raymond has just started his explanation of why this wouldn't work and why we might as well make ourselves comfortable until the museum opens in the morning, when I notice that Fats isn't paying attention. Instead, his nose is twitching and his whiskers are trembling.

"Food," he whispers.

Without another word, he is off across that stone floor. Raymond and I follow, past a phone booth, through an open door, down some steps, along a short hallway to another door. This one is closed. Fats stops in front of it.

My nose isn't as finely tuned as his, but now I smell it too. A tantalizing mix of aromas, from soup to fresh-baked muffins to—can it be?—chocolate chip cookies, that can only add up to one thing. This art museum isn't all bad. It has a restaurant.

Raymond confirms it. Pressing his nose to the glass door, he reads a sign on the wall inside.

"Museum Cafe," he says.

Of course, the Museum Cafe is closed just like the museum. And its glass door is as hard as the floor. But this doesn't stop us. I've infiltrated many a difficult door in my day: heavy wood, screen, revolving, even steel-plated. So I am confident.

The first thing to do is check for cracks. Even the most solid-looking door usually has a crack under it big enough for a mouse to slip through.

I lift the carpet and inspect this door from bottom to top. No obvious cracks or spaces. For just a moment, I am discouraged. Even a hungry Fats can't chew his way through glass. And then I see it. At the bottom, in the corner where the door meets the floor, there is a little chip in the stone. It makes an opening almost too small to notice. But not too small for my sharp eyes. And not too small to squeeze through, I'm sure of it.

This opening is a tight fit. I close my eyes and think of thin things. I am a Pick-Up Stick. I am a strand of spaghetti. I am dental floss. I squeeze my backbone into the thinnest thinness I can imagine. And just like that, I'm inside.

I take a quick look around. The Museum Cafe is a small restaurant, with maybe twenty tables and a counter where food is served. But it looks fully stocked. If we have to spend the night in an art museum, this is the place to be.

"Fats!" I call through the opening. "You're going to love it here."

Eagerly he tries to slip through. But he does not have my agility. He does not have my trim figure. He has Fats's stomach.

"I can't do it!" he wails. "I'm stuck."

I pull. Raymond pushes. Nothing happens.

"Think thin," I urge him. "You are a pencil. You are a string bean. You are thread."

Fats tries. He closes his eyes, sucks in his stomach, and holds his breath, his cheeks puffing out. But it is no use.

Suddenly I have a new idea.

I sniff the air. "I'm not sure," I tell him, "but I think I smell cheese. It could be Swiss or cheddar or muenster. Yes, I do believe it's muenster."

Fats's whiskers wiggle. His eyes grow big.

"Now!" I call to Raymond. I pull as hard as I

can. Raymond pushes as hard as he can. And Fats pops through that hole like a cork from a bottle.

In another moment Raymond is inside, and we are checking out the Museum Cafe. Since it is closed, the food is unfortunately all put away.

"Phooey," mumbles Fats.

But whoever swept the floor today didn't do the best job. Underneath the tables and behind the serving counter we find a crumb of this, a dab of that. An end of roll, a scrap of pretzel, a bite of cookie. A crust of rye bread.

"Cheese!" squeaks Fats. "It's—yes, it's muenster!"

In minutes we have cleaned up that floor. Fats is looking full and a little sleepy. Raymond is yawning too. It's been a long day.

I scout out hiding places and soon find the perfect one. It is under a low cupboard near the kitchen door and next to a trash can. It is a well-known fact that trash cans are a mouse's best friend. Not only are they good to hide behind, but they can be counted on to provide a snack of one kind or another. The parts of kids' lunches they don't like, an occasional pickle, the little ends of ice cream cones, sticky napkins, candy wrappers. Not to mention the odds and ends of junk that Raymond likes to collect.

We pile up a bunch of paper napkins to make a bed. It's not like my cozy canopy bed back at our dollhouse, but it will do for one night.

"Good night," mumbles Fats, pulling a napkin over his head.

In moments, my gang is snoring. But I remain awake, thinking about the day's adventures. I went Outside. I had my first-ever ride in a taxi. I explored Central Park and discovered Rollerblades. I conquered a glass door. And had a tiny taste of muenster. Not bad, I say to myself, even if we are trapped in an art museum.

Not bad at all.

3

I Have
a Big Idea

I wake up in a pile of paper. What is this? I ask myself. Has our dollhouse fallen into a wastebasket while I was sleeping? Then I remember. This is not our dollhouse home. We spent the night in an art museum.

That was a fine adventure. But now it's time to make our escape and take a taxi home.

"Wake up, gang," I order.

Raymond slowly opens one eye. Fats does not stir. Spotting the tip of his tail, I drag him out from under the stack of napkins.

"Where am I?" he squeaks sleepily.

I don't bother to reply.

"It's time to blow this pop stand," I announce. I've been waiting to use that line ever since I heard it in a gangster movie last winter. "As soon as the museum opens, we're out of here."

Raymond jumps to his feet, wide awake. "We need to get out of this restaurant," he says, "and find out when the museum opens. Then the minute people start coming in, we can slip out."

So we go through our thinking-thin, under-the-door exercise again. This time Fats makes it through on the second try.

"I pretended to be a piece of licorice," he says proudly.

Personally, I think it was because he didn't have any breakfast.

In the lobby of the museum, Raymond checks the clock on the wall.

"Eight twenty-eight," he reports. Then he looks at one of the brochures stacked on the Information counter. "The museum opens at nine o'clock. Good, we have half an hour."

While we wait, I check out the little pool at the bottom of the ramp. It is just the right size for a cool swim on a hot day, I notice. Or maybe a sailboat ride. Raymond reads to us about the museum.

"It is called the Solomon R. Guggenheim Museum after the man who started it," he tells us. "The building was designed by a famous architect. And it houses one of the finest collections of modern art in the world."

He goes on to read about the modern art now on exhibit.

"The current exhibit," he says, "is called 'New Visions for the Twenty-first Century.' It includes some of the most talented young artists in the country today. Oh, let's look at the exhibit."

Since we have time to waste, I agree. We walk up the ramp to where the paintings begin.

The first one we see is a bunch of green and yellow squiggles.

"It's a pickle!" says Fats right away. "Oh, I like the Googlestein Museum."

"It's the Guggenheim," corrects Raymond.

"And it's fish swimming," I say. "Or maybe green spaghetti. Or cars on a racetrack."

"It doesn't really have to be anything," Raymond informs us. "This is modern art."

We study the next painting. This one is just a

lot of boxes, black ones and white ones, stacked on top of each other.

"It's a tic-tac-toe game," I say, remembering how we whiled away the long winter nights in the toy department.

"A pile of Eskimo Pies," decides Fats. "Yum! That reminds me. We didn't have any breakfast."

"The interesting thing about modern art," Raymond says in his schoolteacher-ish voice, "is that everyone who looks at it sees something different. Now, what do you see in the next one?"

The next one is even stranger than the first two. This is a picture of nothing. The whole painting is a purple rectangle. Nothing else, not even a box or a squiggle.

Fats is stumped this time. "The artist spilled his grape juice?" he finally guesses.

"What do you think, Marvin?" asks Raymond.

But I hardly hear him. Instead of looking at the purple painting, I am looking at the ramp below it. And instead of seeing grape juice or anything else, I see myself. On Rollerblades. Whizzing all the way from the top of the museum to the bottom. What a ride that would be! Who knows at what high speeds I could travel?

Surely as fast as those skaters in the park. Maybe faster. I might even set a new speed record for land travel by a mouse!

I have had a lot of big ideas in my time, but this one is gigantic. I've got to try it.

"Raymond," I say. "Uh—maybe we don't want to go home quite yet."

When I tell them my idea, my gang does not object. Raymond is happy to continue his study of modern art. Fats is more than happy to take up residence in a restaurant.

"So we will stay at the Googlestein a few more days," I conclude.

"Guggenheim," corrects Raymond.

"Whatever," I say.

The first thing I need, of course, is a pair of Rollerblades.

"No problem," responds Raymond. He prides himself on his ability to improvise anything from his vast collection of found objects. Unfortunately his collection, which takes up an entire room of our dollhouse, is back at Macy's. That doesn't stop Raymond, though. "We just need to go on a little scavenging expedition," he says.

So it is that when the museum opens a few

minutes later, we are hiding under the counter nearest the door, ready to take another trip to Central Park.

It is a snap to dodge between the feet of a slow-moving man with a cane coming in. We pause for just a moment in a patch of ivy outside the door. Then we slip into our disguise—a candy wrapper this time—and make our slow journey down the sidewalk to the traffic light. We cross easily, and in minutes we are back in Central Park.

The first thing I notice, from our observation post under a bench, is how busy it is in the park this morning. It seems as if every family in the city is out for a walk. They are pushing baby carriages and strollers. They are riding bikes and walking dogs. And most of them seem to be all dressed up. Little boys are wearing suits and ties. Little girls are wearing fancy lace dresses.

I nudge Raymond. "What's going on?"

"It's Sunday," he whispers.

Just then I spot something else unusual. A boy carrying a stuffed rabbit. And a girl carrying one of those baskets we saw in Macy's. As she passes by, something rolls under our bench.

Fats pounces on it. "A jelly bean!" he cries.

"Ah." Raymond nods. "Now I understand. It's Easter Sunday."

So this is the big rabbit day. As we watch, a whole procession of them passes by. Little ones dangling from baby carriages. Big ones so enormous, the children can barely carry them. A set of twins have twin rabbits. A little girl pushes a doll carriage filled with rabbits.

Then we see something that makes me blink. It makes Fats's eyes light up and his nose twitch madly. He starts to drool. He jumps up and down with glee.

"A chocolate rabbit!" he squeals. "I must be dreaming. Pinch me and wake me up."

I am glad to oblige. But the chocolate rabbit is still there. It is as large as some of the stuffed ones. And it is sitting in a basket right above us. A little boy in a blue jacket sits on the bench next to it, swinging his feet. Every few minutes he reaches out and breaks off a bite of chocolate.

The smell is driving Fats crazy.

"Drop some," he whispers. "Oh please, drop some."

The little boy is surprisingly neat. He wipes his fingers on a napkin.

"Just a crumb," pleads Fats.

But the boy keeps nibbling and wiping his fingers. He doesn't drop even a tiny crumb.

The rabbit's ears are gone. Now he is working on its foot.

"How can he be so cruel?" Fats whines. "All I want is a little taste." He is kicking his heels on the ground, having a tantrum.

Just then something unexpected happens.

"That's enough chocolate for now, Porter," the little boy's mother says.

"Okay," agrees the boy. He lifts up the basket to walk away. As he does, the chocolate rabbit tips over and falls out. The boy doesn't notice, and neither does his mother. They keep walking.

Fats notices, though. Like a flash, he darts out from under our bench. He grabs that rabbit and starts licking it.

"Fats!" I cry in dismay.

He has lost his mind. He is standing in the middle of a path in the middle of Central Park in broad daylight.

Luckily, no one is passing by. However, that can't last long. Not on the big rabbit day.

"Get back here!" I order.

Suddenly Fats comes to his senses. A look of

panic crosses his chocolate-covered face. He starts trying to drag the rabbit back under our bench. But this rabbit is twice as big as he is. Fats pulls. He pushes. The rabbit doesn't budge.

"You can do it," Raymond calls in encouragement.

Then I see him. The boy has missed his rabbit and come running back to find it.

"Watch out, Fats!" I warn.

He is too busy to see his danger. So I am forced to take drastic action. I launch myself like a rocket and tackle Fats expertly around the knees. I start hauling him back to our bench. But he refuses to let go of the rabbit.

"Drop it!" I growl.

"No!"

Raymond comes out to help. Finally we separate Fats from that rabbit, just as the little boy's hand comes down to pick it up.

Did he see us? Will he start yelling for his mother?

Fortunately for us, all Porter seems to care about is his rabbit. He runs happily back down the path as we collapse under our bench.

"Whew!" sighs Raymond when we all can breathe again. "That was a close call."

"Thanks to Fats." I glare at him, but he doesn't seem to notice.

"I could have had a chocolate rabbit," he whimpers. "A whole entire chocolate rabbit."

He consoles himself with an occasional jelly bean as more families parade by our bench. I keep a watchful eye on him while Raymond proceeds with his mission: gathering materials for my Rollerblades.

What most people call junk Raymond regards as treasure. His favorite activity in the whole world is collecting things humans drop or throw away. He can't believe anyone would get rid of such wonderful stuff. From such useful objects as a bit of wire, a spring, a rubber band, a paper clip, an old flashlight battery, he uses his amazing mechanical brain to build an even more useful object. He has gotten us out of many a tight spot with his inventions. Once he designed a complicated trap to catch a cat. Another time he cracked open a cash register at Macy's. For Raymond, building a pair of Rollerblades will be child's play.

As the minutes and people pass by, I see that familiar gleam in his eye.

"Aha!" He darts out and comes back with a safety pin.

"Would you look at that!" He picks up a button and dusts it off.

"Hmmm. This could be useful." He retrieves a marble from the grass.

I can't see how any of this is going to become Rollerblades, but I am patient.

A paper clip goes into his collection. A hair clip. A Band-Aid. A crayon. A wheel from a toy car.

He gets most excited, though, when a little girl hunting for eggs in the grass (What is that about? I wonder) breaks her necklace. Tiny bright-colored beads fall everywhere. After her family stops hunting for them, Raymond retrieves about a dozen, which he carefully ties up in some plastic wrap.

"Now we're getting somewhere," he tells me.

"We are?"

"Absolutely. Those, Marvin, will be your wheels."

Of course. I knew it all along. What could make better wheels for my Rollerblades than beads? They are just the right size and seem sturdy. And I like the flashy colors too.

But Raymond's best find of the day comes a few minutes later.

He is just packing up his treasures in a baby sock to take back to the museum. I am helping Fats polish off a couple of gourmet-flavor jelly beans. We are arguing about whether the red one is cinnamon or clove when a little shoe drops out of the sky.

"Oh, my," breathes Raymond. He examines it carefully. The shoe is mouse size and made of black plastic.

We look up. Two girls in pink flowered dresses have now taken up residence on our bench. They are playing with their Barbie dolls, undressing them and dressing them up in their Easter finest.

"She should wear her white high heels today," I hear one say.

"Or the gold glittery ones," answers the other.

A moment later, another little black shoe falls into our laps.

"Amazing!" declares Raymond. "A matched pair."

"Perfect," I agree.

We do not linger to see if the two girls will

miss their everyday black Barbie shoes. Raymond stashes them with the rest of his finds. Then he ties a scrap of string around the baby sock, and we are out of there.

Back to the museum, and the start of my great Rollerblading adventure.

4

I Prepare for My Great Adventure

We make ourselves at home in the Museum Cafe. I congratulate myself on my choice of hiding places. No one will ever spot us underneath the cupboard next to the trash can. It is a little noisy for naps in the daytime, when the cafe is always crowded. But the careless sweeper never sweeps there. And he leaves lots of leftovers for our supper.

Fats likes the food here even better than at the gourmet shop in Macy's. The menu is extensive and delicious. In just two days we try six kinds of exotic sandwiches on four exotic breads. We taste a pumpernickel bagel (dry, and hard on the molars), coconut donut (too sweet for me, just right for Fats), blueberry corn muffin (Raymond's favorite), and something called a croissant (it's French, so it must be good). Also pretzels, potato chips, corn chips, and vegetable chips. And for dessert, fruit tarts, cakes, cookies, and brownies. Not just ordinary brownies either. Peanut butter ones. Nutty ones. Chocolate chunk ones. And my own personal favorite: peanut butter pecan chocolate chip.

Fats couldn't be happier, sleeping all day and trying new taste treats all night. Raymond is happy too, as he always is when he is inventing something. He peers through his spectacles at all the junk he has collected. He arranges it in neat little piles. He pulls at his whiskers as he thinks deep thoughts about my Rollerblades.

Finally he gets down to work. I watch as Raymond selects the paper clip from his collection. Using tweezers that fell out of a woman's purse yesterday, he begins to bend the paper clip. He keeps working until he has bent it out of its paper clip shape into one long wire.

"Are they almost ready?" I ask.

"Not yet," replies Raymond.

He bends it back and forth until finally the wire breaks into two same-size pieces. Then he takes the beads from the little girl's necklace and strings three of them onto each wire.

"Now?" I say.

"Patience, Marvin."

That is something I don't have a lot of. But Raymond does. Next he uses the safety pin to make two holes in the bottom of each Barbie shoe. Carefully he pokes the ends of the wire through the holes and bends them so they will stay attached. And just like that, he has made Rollerblades.

"Oh, boy!" I cry. "I'm ready to skate."

"Not quite yet," says Raymond. "First, try them on."

I pull the shoes on easily.

"Perfect," I pronounce.

Raymond helps me stand up. It feels a little strange to be wearing shoes, especially ones that roll. These shoes don't want to stand still. They want to be going somewhere, fast. Just like me.

I take my first step. Right out of my Rollerblades.

"Hmmm." Raymond ponders the situation. "It appears that Barbie has bigger feet than you do."

I think this might be an insult. But before I can reply, Raymond continues, "No problem. We can fix that."

He stuffs the toes of my Rollerblades with bits of shredded napkin.

"Now try them."

With the stuffing, my Rollerblades fit perfectly. At last I am ready for action.

"Stand back, gang," I tell them. "You are about to witness an amazing feat."

"I'm afraid you're still not ready yet," says Raymond.

"I'm not?" What more could I possibly need?

"You can't skate without a helmet."

Oh yes I can, I think. I am bold. I am fearless. I am a finely tuned athlete.

"It's too dangerous. Didn't you see those skaters in the park?" Raymond reminds me. "They were all wearing helmets."

This is true.

"You might fall down and break your head," Fats chimes in.

"Then what would we do?" asks Raymond.

That makes me stop and think. Without me to lead them, this gang would be in deep trouble. Who would bring adventure into their dull, dreary lives? Who would get them out of tight spots with his brilliant ideas? My crafty brain is valuable. Essential, really.

"Oh, all right," I give in.

It takes Raymond another whole day to make me a helmet. First he scavenges a plastic spoon from the top of our cupboard. He tries the bowl part on my head. "Just your size," he tells me. His next step is to remove the handle. He attempts to bend it. He tries to saw it off with a nail file, but the plastic is too tough.

He paces back and forth, thinking. "I've got it!" he exclaims.

As soon as the cafe closes, Raymond runs out and retrieves a salt shaker. He sets it on its side, then lays the spoon across it.

"Marvin, you sit on the handle," he says. "And Fats, I need you to jump into the bowl."

"Jump?" Fats does not favor exercise of any kind.

"Just from the top of the trash can."

Fats looks up. "That is high," he says.

"After you do it," Raymond tells him, "you can go have a nice supper."

"Oh, okay," Fats agrees.

He climbs to the top of the trash can. For a

moment he hesitates. Then, as if he's on a high diving board, he closes his eyes and jumps.

Snap! The spoon breaks neatly at just the right spot.

"Good job, Fats," says Raymond.

Fats doesn't answer. He is lying still with his eyes closed.

"Fats!" Raymond shakes him. "Say something."

Fats opens his eyes. "Can we go have a nice supper now?" he asks.

So we go in search of another gourmet meal. What bread will it be this time? I wonder. That fancy Italian one with olives? A nice pumpernickel? Or perhaps the cinnamon raisin nut bread? And

what fillings? Some roasted this or pickled that? Some new kind of cheese I've never tasted before?

I scamper from table to table. Oddly enough, though, I'm not finding a crust of olive bread or cinnamon raisin or any bread at all. I'm not finding a bite of tart or a bit of jelly donut. I'm not finding the tiniest crumb of peanut butter pecan chocolate chip brownie. When I return to our hiding place under the cupboard, all I bring with me is a dried-up three-day-old raisin.

I see that my gang has done just as poorly. Raymond is nibbling on one sunflower seed. And Fats is holding a limp-looking potato chip.

"I found it under the radiator," he says morosely. "It's probably been there for two weeks. What is going on?"

To my crafty brain, the answer is obvious.

"The sweeper must have really swept," I tell him.

"Or," adds Raymond, "maybe there is a new sweeper. Now that I think of it, I noticed some different shoes out there at closing time. Black, not brown."

Fats ponders the tragedy of it all.

"What if there is a new sweeper?" he says.

"And he sweeps up every single crumb every day? We will starve. We won't be able to stay at the Googlestein. We'll have to go back to Macy's."

"Guggenheim," corrects Raymond.

I am not going back to Macy's. Not until I have skated all the way down that wonderful ramp.

"Maybe our sweeper just had the day off," I suggest.

"Right," agrees Raymond. "We should wait and see who does the sweeping tomorrow. In the meantime, we won't starve. Remember, we have emergency rations."

He goes behind our napkin bed and brings out all the little packets he has collected from the bins on top of our cupboard. There is mustard and mayonnaise and ketchup. Little tubs of butter and jam. And tiny envelopes of sugar, salt, and pepper.

"It's not gourmet," he admits. "However, for tonight it will have to do."

Fats is still looking downhearted. But he rips into those packets as if starvation was just around the corner. Soon he is dipping his potato chip into blobs of mustard and mayonnaise and ketchup, and sprinkling a little sugar on top.

"Not bad," he decides. "You can hardly taste the potato chip at all."

Then he notices the jam.

"Apple, grape, or strawberry?" asks Raymond.

"Strawberry," says Fats.

One dip of his chip into the jam pot, and he is a happy mouse again. In fact, his eyes glaze over and he seems to go into a trance.

"Strawberry jam! Yum yum yummy in my tummy!"

His toes begin to tap. His tail begins to wave.

His stomach begins to jiggle. And he goes into that ridiculous little cheese dance he always does. Only this time it is in honor of jam.

"Jam, jam!" he sings. "Marvelous, glorious, fabulous jam!"

5

I Perform an Amazing Feat

At last I am ready for my big moment. My helmet is firmly attached to my head, protecting my valuable brain. My Rollerblades are securely attached to my feet. I have practiced walking around in them until it no longer feels strange to be on wheels. It feels good. It feels fast and a little bit wild and free.

I stand at the bottom of the ramp, looking at the ceiling far above.

"Okay, gang," I say. "Get ready to witness an extraordinary feat. I shall now skate all the way

from the top of the Googlestein Museum to the bottom."

Fats does not seem impressed. He is busily munching on half an oatmeal cookie that our sweeper, back from his day off, somehow over-looked.

"Guggenheim," corrects Raymond. "You can't do that, Marvin. Not on your first try."

"Why not?" I ask.

Raymond is wearing his worried look again. "You need to practice. Take a trial run down the lower part of the ramp first. See how it feels."

"Nonsense!" I snap. I know how it will feel. It will feel fantastic. This gang of mine has no imagination, no daring. They are holding me back from the greatness that is my destiny.

"I am going up," I tell them. "All the way up."

And just like that, I am off on my big adventure.

Skillfully I make my way up the ramp. Skating uphill, I notice, is more difficult than on level ground. In fact, it is kind of hard work. I feel myself slowing down before I get to the first painting, the one with green squiggles. By the time I reach the one with black and white boxes, I am a tiny bit winded. And when I finally arrive at the grape-juice spill, I hear puffing and panting.

This can't be me, I tell myself. It must be Fats. But, looking down, I see that he is sprawled out comfortably at the bottom of the ramp, still working on his cookie.

I pause to catch my breath.

"Are you all right, Marvin?" calls Raymond.

"Of course," I answer. "Just looking at the painting."

"What do you see?" he asks.

I stare up at that gigantic purple rectangle.

"Hmmm." I think it over. "I see purple clouds

before it rains. I see purple mountains. I see piles of purple plums."

"Very good," says Raymond approvingly. "Now you are beginning to understand what was going on in the artist's mind."

He is really getting into this modern art stuff, I see.

"Or maybe," I add, "he just dropped a can of purple paint."

I resume my climb. Past a painting that looks like the artist threw blobs of every color of paint at it, and another one that looks like the artist wiped off a bunch of brushes on it. And one that looks like the artist lay down and took a nap on it. This canvas has big dents in it. It is long and narrow and mostly gray. What was going on in the artist's mind was he was tired.

I feel the same way. This is like climbing a mountain. It doesn't look so steep up close. But it just keeps going, up and up into the sky. I stand on a small landing, looking toward the ceiling. I figure I have about five more complete circles to go before I reach the top.

I don't really have to go all the way to the top, I think. Not for my first try. I could just take a trial run down the lower part of the ramp and see how it feels. Yes, I decide. That's what I'll do.

"Gang!" I call to them. "Stand back. I'm coming down."

I take a moment to check my equipment, as all good athletes do. My helmet is securely fastened with a rubber band under my chin. My Rollerblades fit snugly and the wheels are in good working order. My nerves of steel are, of course, as hard and tough as ever.

"Are you ready?" I ask.

I look down. Raymond and Fats look very far away. And the ramp seems longer and a little steeper than I expected. My nerves of steel tremble just a tiny bit.

"Ready!" answers Fats.

"Set?" I call.

"Set!" answers Raymond.

"Here I come!"

But I don't move. I notice my knees are shaking.

This is ridiculous. I am Merciless Marvin the Magnificent, after all. I am fearless in the face of danger. I love nothing more than a good adventure. Speed is my life.

"Right now!"

And I push off.

I start slowly. My wheels roll smoothly over the stone floor. This is easy, I tell myself. A piece of cake. In fact, I'm going so slowly that I have time to look at the paintings again. I kind of like the nap one, I decide. It reminds me of Fats after a hearty meal. But the one with all the paint blobs could have used a little more yellow.

As I pass the purple picture, I start to pick up speed. I lean forward and pump my arms like the skaters I saw in the park.

I feel myself going faster. And faster.

This is more like it.

Now I am racing down the ramp. I can hardly see the paintings anymore. They are just a blur of color out of the corner of my eye. But I can see Raymond and Fats. They are getting closer and closer. I must be almost to the bottom.

Raymond is waving his arms at me.

"Slow down, Marvin!" he shouts.

I can't slow down now. I am having too much fun. Rollerblading is every bit as exciting as I thought it would be. Also, it occurs to me that I never practiced slowing down. Not to mention stopping. I have no idea how to do it.

In a flash, I pass Raymond and Fats.

"Watch out!" they cry.

All of a sudden I am aware of obstacles ahead. A hard metal trash can. A hard wooden counter. And beyond that something bright and very hard. The glass front door of the museum.

I have to stop. I try pressing my toes together. I swerve to the left.

I try crossing my feet. I swerve to the right.

But I'm not stopping. I feel like I'm flying through the air.

Oops! I *am* flying through the air.

I am out of control. I do a triple flip and bounce off something. And then, finally, I come to a complete, painful stop.

6

I Discover an Artist

"How are you feeling, Marvin?"

"Can I get you something? A crust of seven-grain bread? It's very healthy. Or a crumb of jelly donut? It's delicious."

I open my eyes to see Raymond and Fats hovering over my napkin bed. How did I get here? I wonder. Why am I lying down? What happened?

Now Raymond is asking more questions.

"What is your name?"

"Merciless Marvin the Magnificent," I mumble.

"Where are you?"

"In the cafe at the Googlestein Museum."

"Guggenheim," corrects Raymond. "In what city?"

"New York, of course."

It is beginning to come back to me now. My magnificent run down the ramp on my Rollerblades. My stupendous wipeout at the bottom. And then Raymond and Fats picking me up and carrying me back to the cafe.

But what is wrong with Raymond? Why is he asking me all these questions?

He nods his head. "Very good, Marvin. Now if you would just wiggle your paws for me."

My paws move easily. My knees, though, are another story.

"Ohhh!" I moan.

Raymond makes a careful examination, bending my knees one at a time, then straightening them out.

"Owww!" I groan.

"Hmmm," he mutters to himself. He takes off his spectacles, polishes them, and puts them back on. "Yes, I think so."

"You think so, what?" I demand.

Raymond straightens up. He looks grave, like the doctor about to deliver bad news to the beau-

tiful young girl in one of those silly old movies we watched last winter on TV.

"Well, Marvin," he says slowly. "I have good news and bad news. The good news is that your brain appears to be in working order, thanks to your safety helmet. The bad news is that your knees are not."

"What's wrong with my knees?"

"I'd say a slight sprain, some bumps and bruises, a few contusions. Nothing seems to be broken, fortunately."

A tiny sprain and a few bumps and bruises aren't enough to keep a tough mouse like me down. I jump out of bed.

"Yowww!" I yelp.

Raymond helps me back into bed.

"You need to rest," he advises. "Just for a couple of days."

So I allow myself to be waited on hand and foot while I recuperate. Raymond brings me a soft pillow made from a little package of tissues. He reads to me from the business pages of the New York *Globe,* which he retrieves each day from the trash can. This enables me to take a lot of naps. Fats keeps offering me new and different snacks left behind by our favorite sweeper. Like a bite of something gooey-sweet that he calls a sticky bun. Or a chip dipped in salsa, a taste sensation so spicy, I feel like I'm about to burst into flame. He even offers to share his greatest treasure, a tiny chocolate rabbit wrapped in foil, which he found under the cash register.

I don't have the heart to take it from him.

"Thanks," I say. "But I think my taste buds need a rest after that salsa."

On the second afternoon, I am resting comfortably, enjoying a dream in which I am skating down the side of the Empire State Building. I am traveling faster than any mouse has ever gone before. Faster than a speeding plane. Faster than a speeding rocket. The wind is in my fur. The bright lights of the city are all around me. This is the life.

Then suddenly something strange happens. Helicopters are buzzing around the building, shining spotlights on me. Policemen with bullhorns are shouting from the street below, "You can't skate on the Empire State Building!" And my beautiful dream turns into a nightmare. Now a giant gorilla named King Kong from another old movie is chasing me. Around and around the building we go. The king of all gorillas comes closer. And closer. I can see his mean, hungry eyes. I can see his terrible teeth. I can see his huge furry paw. It is about to grab me.

"No!" I wake up shivering and shaking.

"What's wrong, Marvin?" asks Raymond. "Are you cold?"

He pulls up another napkin and tucks it around me.

"It was just a bad dream," I tell him.

I sit up, shaking my head to get rid of the

memory of that king-sized gorilla. That is when I notice the napkin covering me. It is the one Fats did his cheese dance on a few nights ago.

"Nice colors," I observe.

"Yes," agrees Raymond. "I especially like the deep mustard yellow. It's vibrant."

"And the bright strawberry pink," I add.

"The design is interesting too," says Raymond. "Just look at the delicacy of those paw prints."

"And the pattern of the tail marks. Really—um—curvy."

Raymond stands back and studies the napkin carefully. He twirls his whiskers as he always does when he is thinking hard. "You know," he says, "I believe this napkin is as good as many of the paintings on display in the museum."

"Better than the one with the squiggles," I put in. "And a whole lot better than the purple paint spill."

"Fats doesn't know it," Raymond goes on, "but he is an artist."

I jump out of bed, my injuries forgotten, to tell Fats the news. This isn't easy to do. He is taking his afternoon nap in his new bed, a paper coffee cup that fell out of the trash can. When Fats takes a nap, it is a serious nap.

"Fats!" I say loudly.

No answer except for a faint snoring sound. *Wheeze-sigh.*

"Wake up!" I command. "We have big news."
Wheeze-sigh. Wheeze-sigh.

"It's about you, Fats," coaxes Raymond.

"Go 'way," comes a muffled voice from inside the coffee cup.

I am forced to take drastic action. I reach in and tickle his toes.

"Stop that! Tee-hee! Oh, that's cruel! Hee-hee-hee!"

Finally we have Fats's attention. He crawls out of the cup, blinking at us.

"Fats," I say, "I have an announcement to make. You will be surprised to hear this. Amazed, in fact. You, a mouse of humble origins, born in the basement of a shoe repair shop on the Lower

East Side, a mouse whose only claim to fame up till now is a mammoth appetite—"

"Yes?" says Fats breathlessly. He has chocolate on his whiskers, I notice.

"You," I conclude with a flourish, "are an artist."

"I am?"

"Oh, yes," confirms Raymond. "We have been looking at this napkin you created. It really is quite remarkable. The colors! The design! Extraordinary!"

Fats looks at the napkin. "It was just a little cheese dance," he says modestly.

"True," agrees Raymond. "But the colors and design are wonderful. You truly are an artist."

"An artist." Fats is wide awake now. A silly grin spreads over his face. "I'm an artist! I always wanted to be something."

"And now you are," I say. "Congratulations."

It is then, at that moment, that I have my brilliant idea.

"A talented artist like yourself shouldn't be hidden away in a coffee cup underneath a cupboard in the Museum Cafe," I tell him. "No, your art should be seen by the world."

"Really?" Fats looks doubtful. "I didn't even use real paint, you know."

"Any artist can use paint," Raymond points out. "Not everyone can create with condiments."

"You must share your talent with the world," I proclaim. "And we will make sure of it. We are going to hang your work on the walls of this museum. Tonight!"

Fats hesitates. "I don't know," he worries. "What if no one likes it?"

"They'll like it better than that dumb purple one," I say.

Fats is still not convinced. "And besides, it smells funny."

I sniff. "It smells delicious. Kind of sweet and sour."

"The smell is just another aspect of the artistic experience," Raymond adds.

I don't know what he's talking about and neither does Fats, I can tell. But he gives in. "Oh, okay."

So that night when the museum visitors and workers have all gone home, we slip once more under the door of the cafe, pulling Fats's rolled-up painting through behind us. We make our way to the bottom of the ramp, scene of my near-triumph and disaster. I don't allow myself to think about that, however. We have to decide where to hang this new contribution to the art world.

I am for placing it near the purple painting. That way people can see which one is the real, genuine, authentic work of art.

Fats is in favor of putting it next to the pickle picture, because he likes the pickle picture.

But Raymond disagrees. "It is a small painting," he reasons. "Therefore we need to hang it where it will be sure to be noticed. I think it should go here at the bottom of the ramp, right under the title of the exhibition."

I have to admit he has a point. Especially when I look up at the large letters that spell out "New Visions for the Twenty-first Century." This is a new vision, all right.

Fats nods. "Okay," he agrees.

Raymond has come prepared for picture-hanging. In his baby-sock knapsack he has several thumbtacks, a safety pin, some odds and ends of string, and a Band-Aid.

He surveys the wall, taps on it a few times, then makes his decision. "I believe it's best to go with the Band-Aid," he mumbles to himself.

I climb on Fats's shoulders. Raymond climbs on my shoulders. He reaches as high as he can. The installation takes only a moment. Then we all jump down and admire the museum's latest work of art.

Raymond is pleased. "Look how the colors stand out against the white wall," he says approvingly.

"Vibrant," I agree.

But Fats is having cold feet again. "Everyone is going to laugh at me," he complains. "I know it. Let's take it down."

"They won't laugh," Raymond reassures him. "They will applaud."

"And besides," I point out, "no one knows you are the artist.

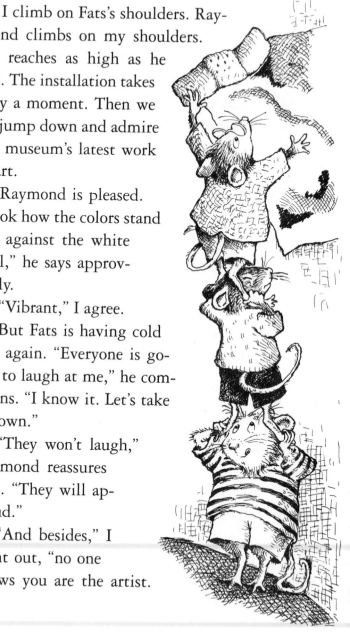

You didn't sign your name. You can't lose. If they laugh, it won't be at you. And if they applaud, you might get to be famous."

Fats brightens up at that.

"So let's wait until tomorrow," suggests Raymond, "and see what happens."

7

I Have a Narrow Escape

Fats wakes me up at the crack of dawn.

"Can we go see yet?" he asks.

"See what?" I mumble crankily. I can't see anything. It feels like the middle of the night.

"See if they like it," he says.

Then I remember. This is the day we find out if Fats is going to be famous.

I jump out of bed. We have a lot to do before the museum opens. Today, for the first time since our arrival, we are going to mingle with the crowd of museum visitors. This could be tricky. It could be dangerous. But I know I, Merciless

Marvin of the Magnificent Brain, can handle it. What we need is an observation post, a safe hiding place in the lobby where we can watch what happens when Fats's painting is discovered.

I tweak Raymond's tail. "No more lazing around in bed," I tell him. "We've got work to do."

We have a quick breakfast of leftover salsa chips, which opens my eyes wide and clears out my nasal passages. Then we are forced to wait while Raymond painstakingly packs up his knapsack.

"What are you taking?" I ask impatiently.

"Just my emergency equipment," he answers. "In case we find ourselves in unexpected danger."

That is the difference between us. I deal with danger by my wits, while Raymond uses his equipment.

He slings his knapsack over his shoulder, and we are on our way.

The clock in the lobby tells us we have a whole hour to wait before the museum opens. This is good. We have plenty of time to check out possible observation posts and choose the best one.

Making a quick survey, I am disappointed to

discover that our choices are limited. This lobby is pretty bare. The only benches are inconveniently located at the opposite end from where we hung Fats's artwork. The only planters are right next to the benches. The counters, where museum workers sell tickets and hand out information, are also too far away.

"Marvin!"

I look at Raymond. His eyes are gazing upward at something I hadn't noticed before.

At the bottom of the ramp, next to the little pool and directly across from Fats's painting, is a tall planter. It is filled with ferns and some kind of little palm tree.

"Gang," I say, "I've got it! The perfect observation post."

We climb up and settle ourselves among the ferns. This is even better than I could have hoped. We are up high, completely removed from the danger of being trampled by museum visitors. The view is fantastic. Also, ferns are soft to sit on.

We have just made ourselves comfortable when my alert ears pick up an unexpected sound: the low buzz of people talking.

Raymond glances at the clock. "Eight forty-five," he whispers.

It is too early for the museum to open. What is going on?

I peer out between the fern fronds. Below us three women and an older man are talking to a young man in a uniform. Another uniformed man stands near the front door. Of course. These aren't visitors but workers getting ready to open the museum.

"It won't be long now," I tell Fats. "Get ready to be famous."

Fats is ready, all right. He is perched on the edge of the planter, a big silly grin on his face, bouncing up and down in anticipation.

We watch the clock as the big hand climbs slowly to the top. Then one of the women nods to the guard. And at last he unlocks the door.

People come streaming in. They are wearing raincoats and carrying umbrellas, along with the usual bags and packages. Children in yellow slickers sit in soggy strollers. It is a rainy day in New York City. Some people sit down on benches or the edge of the pool to wait for friends, while others hurry to the counter to buy tickets. In minutes a line has formed below our planter, waiting for the ticket-taker to let them in to the exhibit.

"This is it!" I whisper in Fats's ear.

We all hold our breath as the first visitors, a young couple, hand their tickets to the ticket-taker.

And walk right past Fats's painting to the elevator.

"Ohhhh," Fats sighs in disappointment.

Raymond shakes his head. "They didn't even notice."

I can't believe it. This is an art museum. Can't these visitors see art right in front of them? What is wrong with their eyes?

"Hmmph," I mutter. Then it occurs to me that maybe something *is* wrong with their eyes. "Maybe they need glasses," I speculate.

After the young couple come three elderly ladies.

They too walk right by Fats's work of art.

"Phooey," mumbles Fats.

"Maybe they need new glasses," I suggest.

More and more visitors go in.

"Come on," I coach them under my breath. "Walk slowly. Now open your eyes and look around. To the right, down near the floor. No, not there, you dodo!"

More and more visitors walk right by.

I shake my head in disgust. "You know what's wrong with these people?" I say to my gang. "They haven't woken up yet."

But Raymond disagrees. "It's all my fault," he says. "I should have hung the painting higher. And I should have made a nice frame for it."

Fats, meanwhile, has gone into a major mope.

"I knew it," he moans. "It was a crazy idea. I'm not an artist, only a hearty eater. I didn't even use real paint."

"You *are* an artist," Raymond tells him. "You just haven't been discovered yet. Think of the great artists of the past. Some of them had to wait years to be discovered. You have to be patient."

But Fats refuses to listen. As usual, when the going gets tough, his thoughts turn to food.

"Just think," he says. "Right now someone might be dropping a piece of coconut donut next to our trash can. Let's go see."

"We can't do that," I reply. "Look at all the people down there."

"But I'm hungry," he complains.

"Too bad!" I snap.

"Charming," says someone. "Simply charming."

"Marvin! Fats!" whispers Raymond. "Look at this."

Fats and I stop arguing and look down.

A young woman is stooped over next to Fats's painting. She has just finished tying a little girl's shoe. Now a man leans over.

"Oh my, yes," he says. "Harold, Marge, did you see this little painting?"

Another man and woman come over.

"Lovely," says the woman. "Look at those tiny brush strokes."

"And the rich colors," adds the man.

More people join the circle that is beginning to surround Fats's work.

"So delicate," sighs an elderly lady.

"And yet so strong," says another.

"Just wonderful!" someone else is saying. "But I don't see it listed in the catalog. Who is the artist?"

"Me!" cries Fats, waving his paws.

I can't believe my eyes. "Shhhh!" I hiss at him.

"Fats!" Raymond is shocked.

But Fats pays no attention. "Here I am!" he calls, bouncing up and down.

"What are you thinking of?" Raymond tugs at his sleeve, trying to pull him down. "We are mice, remember? Have you forgotten what people do when a mouse calls attention to himself?"

Fats, though, is out of control. "I am the artist!" he shouts. "Up here! In the ferns!"

"What they do," warns Raymond, "is call the Exterminator."

The dreaded word stops Fats in mid-bounce. A look of terror crosses his face.

At that moment I make a grab for him.

But he slips out of my paws. For a second he teeters on the edge of the planter. He tries to hold on to a fern, but it breaks. And before I can reach out to save him, he falls.

"Fats!" cries Raymond.

I brace myself for what will happen next. The screams, the running feet, the angry faces of the museum guards—and yes, even the appearance of the terrible Exterminator.

Nothing happens.

Carefully concealing myself in the fern fronds, I peer down into the lobby. Oddly enough, everything appears to be normal. People are still milling around with their umbrellas. The guard still stands near the front door. The ticket-sellers are still selling tickets. The ticket-taker is still taking tickets. A small group is still gathered around Fats's painting.

But where is Fats?

He is not lying in a broken heap on the floor. That is good. He is not bobbing around in the pool. He hasn't landed in the lap of someone sitting on the edge of the pool. Or has he?

My sharp eyes study a man in a raincoat and hat reading a newspaper. No Fats in the hat. No Fats in the folds of the newspaper. But what about the woman next to him? She is eating something from a brown bag in her lap. Could Fats have been lucky enough to land in a bag of jelly donuts?

The woman takes a last bite, then scrunches

up the bag and goes to find a trash can. No Fats in the bag.

Raymond and I look at each other. Where can he be?

The only other people sitting by the pool are a mother and little boy. The boy is kicking his feet restlessly against the wall. He doesn't seem too happy to be at an art museum. His backpack sits next to him. Sticking out of the top, I can see the heads of a stuffed elephant and a stuffed tiger. No Fats in the backpack.

Raymond nudges me. "Look at that," he whispers.

I look where he is pointing.

The elephant's ear is moving.

Are my eyes playing tricks on me? I look again. No, it's true. One of the elephant's ears is slowly flapping in the breeze. Only there is no breeze. It is a signal—from Fats.

Once again I congratulate myself on my years of skillful training, which have taught Fats all he knows. Then I notice that his tail is sticking out. We've got to get him out of that backpack before he is discovered.

But how? I think of all the rescue missions I've seen in the movies. A helicopter would be good right now. We could hover over the back-pack, then drop a rope ladder and Fats could climb to safety. Or how about a parachute jump into the pool, followed by an underwater rescue? In the dark of night, of course.

"Uh-oh." Raymond pokes me again. "Trouble."

It seems that the woman and little boy were waiting for someone. And she has arrived. Grandma. Now they are hugging and talking. But in a minute they will be handing their tick-ets to the ticket-taker and disappearing, never to be seen again. And Fats will go with them.

This is an emergency. Raymond, I see, is unfas-tening his knapsack. Inside is a strange assortment of objects that he has collected from the floor of the cafe in the last few days. Three marbles, two checkers, a subway token, four pennies, and a quarter.

"What are those for?" I ask.

"This," answers Raymond, "is a distraction."

He hands me the checkers and the pennies. "We throw all this stuff down near the boy," he says. "Then while he and everyone else nearby are distracted, we steal Fats out of the backpack."

It could work. Anyway, we don't have time for my other, more exciting plans.

"On the count of
three," says Raymond.
"One . . . two . . .
three!"

We toss out the
distractions. And,
amazingly, it
works. The boy
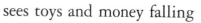
sees toys and money falling
from the sky and goes after it. His mother and
grandmother go after him. Everyone nearby is
looking at the commotion. No one is looking at
the backpack.

Like lightning, I am down from the planter
and into that backpack, with Raymond close behind.

We grab Fats from behind the elephant's ear.

"Let's go!" I say.

Off we race across the lobby, zigzagging
between umbrellas and strollers and shopping
bags, zipping from counters to benches. It is a
hair-raising journey, filled with near-collisions,
near-tramplings, and near-discovery. But I am, as
always, just one step ahead of disaster. We pause
in an empty phone booth to catch our breath,
then weave between umbrellas, boots, and pack-

ages down the little hallway to the trash can outside the Museum Cafe.

Darting behind it, we collapse into a puffing, panting, exhausted pile. Here we will stay until the museum closes.

"Marvin," says Fats when he can finally speak.

"What?" I ask.

"Thanks for saving me."

"It was nothing," I answer. "Just another daring, heroic rescue operation."

He is quiet for a few minutes. I think he has gone to sleep.

"Marvin," Fats says again.

"What?"

"I am an artist."

Fats grins happily. Then he closes his eyes and starts to snore.

8

I Discover a Very Talented Artist

Now that Fats knows he is an artist, he is a new mouse. He can't wait to get started on new paintings. The very next morning, he is hard at work with his mustard and mayonnaise and ketchup packets and his little jelly tubs.

He performs his famous cheese dance as he has never done it before, with new words this time. "I'm an artist—hooray!" he shouts. "An artist— hooray! An artist, an artist, an artist—hooray!"

In one day Fats produces six new works of art.

But when he spreads them out to look at them that night, he makes a disappointing discovery.

"They all look alike," he sighs.

For the first time that day, Fats is not smiling.

"Not exactly," I reassure him. "The ones where you used grape jelly are more purple. And the strawberry ones are more red."

"Condiments do limit your colors, though," Raymond observes.

Fats nods. "I don't have any green or blue," he complains. "Or turquoise or tangerine or hot pink. I don't even have any black. A painter really needs paint."

"Paint. Hmmm." Raymond takes off his spectacles, carefully polishes them with a scrap of napkin, then puts them back on. I can practically hear the wheels turning inside his brain as he thinks over the problem. "A black pen would be easy," he says. "I almost got one yesterday, but then a man picked it up. And someone might drop a hot-pink lipstick. But a whole set of paints? Not very likely."

"Hmmm." Fats puts on a thinking face like Raymond's. "I know! Maybe we could find paints in the park."

Paints in the park. It sounds good. But then I remember all the time we spent under that park bench on Easter Sunday. I didn't see a single human carrying a paint set.

I have a better idea. "We'll raid a paint store!" I announce. "Uh, I mean, an art store."

That gets their attention. I can see it all now, just like in the movies. In the dark of night we glide from shadow to shadow through the city streets, skillfully avoiding policemen and stray cats. Finally we arrive at the Famous Artists art store. Naturally it is locked up tight, not only by a sturdy door, but a steel gate covering the front.

But this doesn't bother me. Slipping between the slats of the gate, I case the joint. And right away I spot the only possible way to get inside: the mail slot. "I'm going in," I tell my gang. I slip easily through the slot. And step right on the wire of a burglar alarm.

But this doesn't bother me. Using my special wire-cutters, I cut that wire just in time, before it can call the cops. I survey the store, looking for paints. I don't have to look far. This store is filled with so many kinds of paints, I don't know which to choose. Then I spot some super-fancy paint sets inside a glass case. Only the best is good enough for an artist like Fats. There is only one problem. The case is locked.

But this doesn't bother me. Taking out my lock-picking tools, I pick that lock in a matter of seconds. I grab the biggest, best, most expensive-looking paint set and start to make my getaway. Nothing to it, I'm thinking—until I get to the front door. How am I going to fit that biggest, best paint set through a little mail slot?

But this doesn't bother me . . .

"Marvin?" Raymond rudely interrupts my daydream.

"Huh?"

"I was just saying that raiding an art store is one possibility. But it would take time and careful preparation. Artists work with many different kinds of materials, you know. Why don't we take another look at the exhibit? Fats can see what else they use besides paint."

"Yes!" says Fats.

I like my plan better. But I guess taking another look at the exhibit wouldn't hurt. And we can do it now, right this minute.

So off we go on a museum tour. We climb all the way up the ramp to the top, near the ceiling, and look at each picture going down. After the first few, I lose interest. All these artists use is paint, gobs and gobs of it. I see paint splashed on and spattered on and slathered on. I see paint in turquoise and tangerine and hot pink and all the other exotic colors Fats could imagine. I get tired of looking at paint.

Instead, I look down the long, winding, spiraling ramp and imagine myself going down it on Rollerblades. Flying down this runway at supersonic speed. I have to do it. I was born to do it. Only first I need to learn how to stop.

"Come on, gang," I say. I've had enough of this art stuff. I want to go practice my skating.

But Raymond and Fats are dawdling far behind. Looking back, I see them standing in front of a piece of art I barely glanced at.

"Move it along," I urge.

"Just a minute, Marvin," calls Raymond.

Fats doesn't say anything. He is staring at this picture as if he's in a trance.

I can see I'm going to have to drag them out of here. As I get closer, though, I see why Fats is staring. This art is not made from paint. It is made out of a bunch of junk: little pieces of wood, cardboard tubes, folded newspaper, scraps of torn cloth. The more I look at it, the more materials I see. Wire hangers, bits of broken glass, a china tea cup, even part of a toothbrush.

"What kind of crazy art is this?" I ask.

"It is called a collage," Raymond the Art Expert informs me. "This is a technique where the artist combines various kinds of materials."

"I could do that," Fats says softly.

I stand back to get a better view. This collage thing has a mixed-up look. It is kind of bright, but kind of dull. It is kind of quiet, but kind of busy. It is kind of brown, but not really. I can't figure out what was going on in this artist's mind. I look at the title. "Number 38." That helps a lot.

"I could do that," Fats says again. That big silly smile has returned to his face.

"Well," I say. "Why don't you?"

Fats goes right to work, ripping up things. For two days he tears up everything in sight: napkins, of course, salt and pepper packets, tea bags, straw wrappers, the tops of jelly tubs, mustard and mayonnaise and ketchup packets. He collects found objects our careless sweeper has left behind: candy wrappers, a lollipop stick, potato chip bags, a Cracker Jack box. And the best prize of all: a hot-pink Dubble Bubble gum wrapper.

All of these are torn into a million pieces.

"This is fun!" Fats crows happily.

I give him some help with the Cracker Jack box, and I have to admit I agree. This collage thing isn't bad.

In the meantime Raymond is busy darting in and out, bringing in some fine white powder, mixing it up with water. The result is a mysterious concoction in a coffee cup.

"What is that?" I ask.

"This," replies Raymond, "is a simple white

paste. I made it from flour I found spilled on the kitchen floor, and water."

He also has another surprise for Fats.

"You will need something sturdy to glue your ripped pieces onto," he says. "I've been trying to find some cardboard, but all I could come up with was this envelope."

It is an odd shape, long and thin, but it seems sturdy. Anyway, it is stronger than a napkin.

Fats doesn't care what shape it is. He can't wait to start gluing.

"Thanks, Raymond," he says.

Fats has as much fun gluing as he did ripping. Maybe more. Pretty soon everything in sight is covered with white paste. Even my napkin bed is sticky. When Raymond and I go to sleep that night, Fats is still working on his collage. And when I wake up the next morning, I feel something stuck to my nose.

"Dubble Bubble! Ha, ha, ha!" Fats is pointing and laughing.

I give him my most evil glare.

"Uh, sorry, Marvin." Fats unglues my nose. "I finished my collage. Come and see."

Fats must be an artist. He has taken a bunch of

ripped paper and glued it all over an envelope and it looks good.

"I like the colors," I tell him. "They're vibrant."

"The hot pink makes it, don't you think?" says Fats modestly.

"The textures of all the different materials are pleasing," Raymond adds. "And the pattern of light and dark is quite interesting."

"I thought so," agrees Fats.

"I like it a lot better than Number Thirty-eight," I say. "What are you going to call it?"

"Hmmm." Fats thinks it over. "How about Number Two?"

We install Number 2 next to Fats's condiment picture that very night. Getting it through the hole under the door is a little tricky, and a couple of pieces fall off, but that doesn't bother Fats. He is not a fussy artist. He just sticks them on again.

And the next morning we are once more at our observation post, waiting to observe the reaction of the museum visitors. This time Fats has promised to behave himself. He will not shout, wave, or bounce. To be on the safe side, though, Raymond and I both have a firm grip on his tail.

We wait patiently while the museum workers

arrive and have their morning chat. We wait while the front door opens and visitors start coming in. No umbrellas this time, I observe. It is a sunny day in New York City. We wait while they stand in line to buy their tickets, and then, finally, hand them to the ticket-taker.

Either today's visitors have sharper eyes or they have heard about the mystery artist. Because in just a few minutes, a little crowd begins to gather around Number 2. We strain our ears to hear what they are saying. I catch fragments of their comments. "Lovely colors." "Interesting textures." "Pattern of light and dark." And then a tiny gray-haired lady claps her hands. "Delightful!" she says.

"They like it!" Fats sighs.

A minute later something unexpected happens. The crowd is joined by three new people, two women and a man. They don't appear to be ordinary visitors. They look very serious, and all three of them wear little badges on their jackets.

"Do you see the woman with the black hair?" Raymond whispers excitedly. "She is the museum director. I saw her picture in the information brochure. The others must be her assistants."

They act like art experts. They stand back. They look for a long time at Fats's collage. They frown. They walk back and forth, studying it from every angle. They frown some more. They don't say anything.

"They hate it!" Fats whimpers.

The woman with the black hair turns and says something very quietly to the man. Unfortunately, we can't hear what it is.

The man studies Fats's collage for another long minute. Then he nods.

"Yes," he says. "I agree. Whoever this mystery artist is, he or she is very talented."

"Did you hear that?" I say to Fats.

He heard it, all right.

"*Very talented!* That's me!"

Forgetting all his promises, he is squealing and waving and bouncing like a Ping-Pong ball.

Raymond and I not only have to sit on his stomach but gag him. Finally, when he has completely subsided into the ferns, I allow him to speak.

"Very talented!" he repeats. "Isn't it amazing?"

9

I Perform a Fabulous Feat

"Very talented."

That is all I hear for the next few days. Fats repeats it to himself while he works happily on his latest artistic creations. He loves making collages. He constructs one that consists of nothing but mustard packets. His colors aren't so vibrant this time, but Raymond and I admire the way he arranges them in the shape of a hot dog. After a lot of thought, he decides to call it Number 3.

Then he moves on to a collage with a candy theme. Not only does Fats use candy wrappers for this one, but actual candy besides. This is a great sacrifice for a hearty eater like Fats. I see him contemplating half a roll of Life Savers, which Raymond found under the table in the far corner.

"To eat or to glue?" he wonders out loud. "That is the question."

I'm not surprised when he decides to eat. But the Life Savers turn out to be spearmint, his least favorite flavor.

"Brrrr." He shivers as the cool, minty flavor takes his breath away. "I think I'll glue."

He also collects a couple of dusty M&M's, a twist of licorice, some old lollipop sticks, and a squashed pink jelly bean. The jelly bean gives him another moment of agonizing, paw-wringing indecision.

"Pink is one of my favorite flavors," he observes. He sniffs the jelly bean. He takes a tiny lick of one end. "But I need a touch of pink in that corner. Oh, dear, what shall I do?"

Then, amazingly, he commits an act of huge self-sacrifice.

"I'll glue," he decides.

That is when I realize that Fats has become a true artist.

When it comes to gluing on candy, Raymond's white paste doesn't work so well. The jelly bean falls off three times. Fats is so disappointed, he again considers eating it. But Raymond, as usual, comes up with a solution to the problem: used chewing gum. He collects it from under the tables and chairs where little kids have sat.

"Perfect for attaching heavy objects," he declares.

A little dab of gum, and that jelly bean is firmly attached.

Meanwhile, I have other things on my mind. Namely, my next Rollerblading adventure. But before I undertake another run, it is crucial that I learn how to stop. What I need, I decide, is a practice ramp. So while Fats and Raymond glue candy, I use my powerful brain to devise one.

I survey the Museum Cafe for a suitable slanted surface. At first, nothing strikes my eye. All the furniture is straight up and down, like chair legs, or straight across, like tabletops. Then my eye happens to fall on a stack of trays on a small table near the door. Customers slide these trays along the counter, load food on them, then carry them to their table. Propped up on one end, what could be more perfect for a mouse-size ramp?

All I need to do is retrieve one. This will

not be easy. Climbing to the top of the stack, then lowering down a tray will take all my well-developed muscles and ingenuity.

"Hmmm." I pace up and down, waiting for a brilliant idea to strike.

Once again, the careless sweeper comes to the rescue. Part of his job is to collect clean trays and stack them up for the next day. However, I notice, he missed a couple. Fortunately for me, he left them leaning against a table leg.

"Bingo!" I exclaim.

Using all my well-developed muscles, I drag one of those trays back to the cupboard that has become our temporary home and art studio. I zip up to the coffee machine and zip down with two empty paper coffee cups. I place them under one end of the tray and—presto!—I have my ramp.

I begin practicing immediately. For many hours I race down that ramp on my Rollerblades, trying to stop at the bottom. I accumulate more bumps and bruises and a contusion or two. But finally I think I've got the hang of it. It's all in the foot action, I discover. You have to apply pressure on the side of the wheels so they dig into the floor.

"Hey, gang. Watch this!" I say.

I give them a demonstration, with a nifty little turn thrown in at the end for good measure.

"Hooray!" cheers Fats.

"I think you've got it," says Raymond.

I know I have.

"I'm ready," I tell them. "Tomorrow is the night. And this time I am going to skate from the top of the Googlestein to the bottom."

Raymond the Worrier looks alarmed, as usual.

"Guggenheim," he corrects. "You'll wear your safety helmet."

"Of course."

"And your knee guards."

"Knee guards?"

"Just a minute."

Raymond the Collector disappears under the cupboard. A minute later he emerges from his junk corner with two Mickey Mouse Junior Band-Aids. "These will protect your knees."

"Oh, okay," I agree.

So the next night, just as soon as the museum closes, I am ready for my big moment. I am wearing my safety helmet and my new knee guards with the Mickey Mouse faces on them. But not my Rollerblades. One thing I learned from my last attempt was that it's easier to walk up that long ramp on your feet than on Rollerblades. I say good-bye to Raymond and Fats, who will be waiting down below.

"Not that we don't think you can stop," Raymond assures me. "But just in case."

Up, up, up I climb in a long curling spiral until at last I reach the top, close to the glass ceiling. I pause there for a moment's rest. Climbing the Googlestein is kind of like climbing a mountain. Only when you get to the top, you don't see blue sky and sparkling lakes and other mountains in the distance. All you see is paintings.

I strap on my Rollerblades. Then I pause again to check my equipment. My little wheels are rolling easily. My helmet and my knee guards are nice and snug. I am ready to roll.

I take a look down the long ramp. Because of all the curves, I can't see the bottom. I can't see Raymond and Fats. All I can see is stone floor and curving walls. And paintings, of course. But I know what thrills and excitement are waiting for me.

"Here I come!" I call, even though I know Raymond and Fats can't hear me. "Right now!"

And off I go.

Just as before, I start slowly. I push with my

legs and pump with my arms to gather speed. As I round the first turn, I feel myself starting to go faster. And faster still. The paintings go rushing by in streaks of green and purple, turquoise and tangerine. Was that Number 38 I just passed? I can't tell, I am going so fast.

But I want to go even faster. I lean forward and pump harder, picking up more speed. Around curves and down straightaways I go on my flying feet. I can't see anything now. I only feel the world whizzing by. And I laugh out loud. This must be what it's like to be a jet plane. I am Supersonic Marvin. I am traveling faster than the speed of sound. Or is it light?

The faster you go, the sooner the ride is over. That is a little rule of mathematics that Raymond didn't need to teach me. I figured it out all by myself. So in no time, I sense that I am nearing the bottom.

I round another curve. Suddenly I see Raymond and Fats waving at me.

"Rats," I say to myself. My wonderful ride is over.

I don't want it to be over.

"Slow down!" calls Raymond.

I don't want to slow down.

With a casual little wave of my paw, I zoom past them.

Now I hear them both shouting behind me. "Stop, Marvin!"

I don't want to stop.

"The door!"

Suddenly I see that hard glass front door looming in front of me. Uh-oh. I remember my last encounter with that door. I don't think I want to do that again.

I better stop, I decide.

I slam on the brakes with all

my might. My Rollerblades squeal, and I hear a strange popping sound. Then I come to a screeching halt, just an inch from the front door.

"Oh, wow!" cries Fats. "What a ride!"

"Are you all right?" worries Raymond.

They are both standing over me as I get to my feet.

"All right?" I say. "I've never been better."

10

I Make
Fats Famous

"Tell me again," I say.

"You were going so fast, I almost couldn't see you," repeats Fats.

I smile. "And?"

"And I didn't know how you were going to stop. It looked like for sure you were going to crash into the door."

"But?"

"But you didn't. You made a spectacular last-second stop."

"Thank you," I say modestly. "It *was* pretty spectacular."

It is the next morning, and I am reclining on my napkin bed, reliving my triumph of last night. Raymond is over in his junk corner trying to repair my left Rollerblade, which didn't quite survive my spectacular stop. That sound I heard was the bead wheels popping off the wire. And Fats is hard at work on his newest collage.

I have replayed my fabulous feat in my mind a hundred times. The thrill of whizzing down that ramp at a zillion miles an hour, undoubtedly breaking the world speed record for travel by a mouse. The hair-raising split-second of alarm when I saw the glass door in front of me. And the skillful athletic maneuver that brought me to my spectacular stop an inch from disaster. My heart beats faster just thinking about it.

But mixed in with all the excitement is a tiny touch of a letdown. Now that I have climbed the mountain—and raced down it—what will I do next? After you break the world speed record, what do you do for an encore?

Maybe I could try bicycle racing. Or stock-car racing. Or . . . I wonder if there is such a thing as jet plane racing.

I am just having a little daydream in which I am hurtling through the sky at twice the speed of sound—or is it light?—leaving all the other jet planes stuck in a cloud, when I hear Fats say, "It's finished."

I blink. "What's finished?"

"Number Five," he answers. "What do you think, Marvin?"

I can see right away that Number 5 has an ice cream theme. It is covered with Popsicle sticks and Italian ice wrappers and ice cream cup covers. And even some ends of real cones, which Fats must have found in the trash can. No real ice cream, though.

"It's—uh—vibrant," I tell him.

"Full of contrasting textures," adds Raymond.

"Delicious?" asks Fats hopefully.

"Absolutely delicious," Raymond pronounces.

Fats can't wait to hang his latest tasty creations. However, now that he is working with real food, we have a little problem. How can we get Numbers 3, 4, and 5 through the hole under the door?

"They can't be rolled up," says Raymond, shaking his head. "Or folded. It can't be done."

"Well, then," I decide. "We'll just have to go through the door. When it is open."

Raymond looks horrified.

"Not during the day," I reassure him. "At closing time."

"How can we do that?" he asks.

"You'll see," I say.

So that night, when all the visitors have gone home and only the careless sweeper is left in the Museum Cafe, we slip out from under our cupboard. Sticking to the shadows, we scurry from counter to table to chair leg until we reach the little table where the trays are stacked. There, next to the closed door, we wait.

"What if he doesn't open the door?" Fats whispers.

"He's got to go home sometime," I point out.

Raymond is looking nervous.

"What if he sweeps under this table?" he asks.

"He never has before."

As if to illustrate my point, Fats sneezes.

"Shhhh!" I cover his mouth with my paw.

"Sorry," he whispers. "It's dusty under here."

I peer out to make sure we haven't been detected. That is when I notice something rather peculiar. The careless sweeper is carelessly sweeping around the round table closest to us. While he sweeps, he sways and smiles and kind of dances with his broom. What is that about? I wonder.

And then I notice something else. He is wearing headphones. And suddenly I understand. He is listening to music while he sweeps.

This brings a smile to my face. His mind is not on his work. No wonder he misses all those treats we get to eat. This sweeper is our best friend, I decide. He is my favorite human in all the world.

"Gang," I say. "This is going to be easy."

And it is. The careless sweeper finishes his sweeping, still listening to his music. He opens the door, still swaying to his music. He pauses for a moment, his eyes closed, still dancing to his music.

That is all we need.

We dart through the open door. And off we go to add Numbers 3, 4, and 5 to Fats's exhibit.

Numbers 3, 4, and 5 are a big success.

From our observation post on high, we observe the crowd that gathers around them the next morning. It is much bigger than last time. Word must be spreading about the museum's mystery artist. The museum director comes again, this time with four assistants trailing behind her. And a photographer. And several other Very Important People. We can tell they are important by the way they pace up and down in front of Numbers 3, 4, and 5, looking at them from every angle, mumbling to themselves, and jotting down notes in little notebooks.

"Why are they doing that?" whispers Fats.

Raymond thinks it over. "I know!" he says excitedly. "They must be art critics."

The highlight of Fats's day comes when one of those Very Important People stops in front of Number 4, the candy collage. He remains motionless, studying it carefully, for about fifteen minutes. Then he straightens up. He turns to another of the Very Important People and says, just loud enough for us to hear, "It's a little jewel."

Anticipating big trouble, I immediately grab

for Fats's tail. But he appears to have learned his lesson. He does not wave, shout, or bounce. He just smiles.

"I'm a little jewel," he sighs.

My own personal highlight comes a few minutes later. I am beginning to get bored with all this art stuff. I gaze up the ramp, remembering my speedy trip down it only a few hours ago. Did all of that really happen? I ask myself. Or was it just a wonderful, fantastic dream?

That is when it hits me. I notice the railing that winds along the last curve of the ramp, ending with a sudden drop at the bottom. And I think, Ski jump!

During the depths of last winter, when even my favorite old gangster movies on TV were starting to get boring, Fats discovered winter sports. Downhill ski racing. The giant slalom. The two-man bobsled. These were my kind of sports: fast, dangerous, exciting. But most exciting of them all, I decided, was ski jumping. What could be better than racing down a runway at around a hundred miles an hour, then jumping out into space? The ski jumpers soared high in the air, floating in the sky like birds before gliding down for a graceful landing.

I can do this, I think. With my Rollerblades as skis and the railing as a mouse-size runway, I too can become a ski jumper.

"Yes!" I shout.

Raymond and Fats stare at me in shock.

"Marvin!" says Fats.

"Have you gone crazy?" asks Raymond.

With a tremendous effort, I get ahold of myself. I sit down quietly.

"Not crazy," I tell them. "Not crazy at all."

The next morning I reveal to them my latest plan.

"So you see," I finish. "In just a few days, I will perform a new and daring feat."

I wait for their reaction. Fats, I am sure, will cheer. And Raymond will disapprove, fearing for my safety.

Neither of them says a word.

I look at Fats. Obviously, he has not been paying attention. He is deep in thought, a foolish little grin on his face. Either he is telling himself again that he is a talented little jewel or he is deciding what materials he'll use for Number 6. Or maybe he is just thinking about lunch.

Raymond's nose is buried in his morning newspaper. This is strange. Maybe he didn't hear me.

"It's going to be dangerous," I say, raising my voice. "Extremely dangerous."

"That's nice," Raymond mumbles without looking up.

What in the New York *Globe* could be more interesting than me?

"Fascinating," he says to himself. "Oh my, would you look at that."

"Look at what?" I demand.

"This story in the newspaper. It's about Fats."

"What?"

In an instant, Fats and I are both looking over his shoulder.

"There's a picture!" I exclaim.

"Of Number Four!" Fats can't believe it. "Oh wow, it's me! I'm in the newspaper! That's my collage. I made it out of real candy. Oh, I'm glad I used that pink jellybean. I didn't really want to, you know, but I did."

Raymond interrupts his little celebration. "There is quite a nice story here too."

"Read it! Oh, please read it," begs Fats.

Raymond pushes his spectacles back on his nose and begins to read.

"Mystery at the Guggenheim Museum." He pauses. "That's the headline," he explains. Then he con-

tinues, *"Museum officials are puzzled and intrigued today by five small works by an unknown artist that have suddenly appeared on the walls of their latest exhibit, 'New Visions for the Twenty-first Century.' Four of the five are collages, made of paper and found objects, and all are unsigned. According to Guggenheim Museum Director Marguerite Devereux, 'The works are meticulously crafted and are obviously the work of an extremely talented artist.'"*

"Extremely talented!" Fats repeats. "Extremely is even better than very, isn't it?"

"I'd say so," confirms Raymond.

He goes on to read comments from the Very

Important People we saw looking at Fats's work yesterday. *"Brent Montague of* Modern Art Review *told this reporter that he considers the collage pictured above to be 'a little jewel.' He also noted that all the collages on display have a food theme and called this 'a comment on America's food-obsessed society.' And Adriana Fabini, Curator of Special Collections for the Museum of Modern Art, summed up the works as 'miniature marvels.'"*

"Miniature marvels! Yippee!"

Fats is so beside himself, I'm afraid he is going to rush out into the middle of the Museum Cafe and announce it to the world.

"Fats," I say in my sternest voice. "Calm down."

He pays no attention.

"Hee-hee!" he crows, going into his bouncing routine again. He looks like he's on an invisible pogo stick. "A jewel and a marvel, that's me!"

"Fats," I warn. "I have just one word to say to you." I lean close and whisper it slowly in his ear. "Ex-ter-min-a-tor."

He quiets down quickly at that. "What else does the story say?" he asks in his normal voice.

"The rest of the story is about who this mystery artist might be," says Raymond. "The director thinks it could be an artist who was upset about being left out of the exhibit. But, she says, she cannot identify any known artist who works on such a small scale. Also, she is mystified at how the artist managed to hang the pieces on the wall without being observed. Because of this, she speculates that it might be a member of the museum staff."

"Good thinking," I say.

"And here is the last sentence," Raymond concludes. *"Ms. Devereux expressed hope that the unknown artist will now come forward to reveal his or her identity and solve this unusual museum mystery."*

"Okay," says Fats.

"Okay what?" I ask.

"Okay, I'll come forward and solve the mystery."

I can't believe this. I am forced to sit on his stomach and give his tail a little sample of my torture twist.

"All right," Fats whimpers finally. "I give up."

I let go of his tail. "Now," I say, "repeat after me."

"I know," he interrupts with a loud sigh. "Exterminator, Exterminator, Exterminator."

11

I Lead a Raid
on Central Park

Fats is so excited about being in the newspaper, he insists that Raymond read the article to him again. And again. By the end of the day, he practically knows it by heart. He even rips the article out of the paper so he can sleep with it under his pillow.

"What part did you like best?" he asks me. "Where they said I was extremely talented, not just very? Or where they said my collages were miniature marvels? Or did you prefer the part about the little jewel?"

"Actually," I say, "my favorite part was where

they said your art was all about food and that says something about society. I can't say I agree."

"You can't?"

"No," I reply. "What it says about society is *you* like to eat."

"Oh." Fats seems disappointed. He retreats to his coffee-cup bed. I think he is going to sleep. Then he pokes his head out again.

"I could say something else about society," he says.

"What could you say?" I ask.

"I don't know yet," he answers. "I'm going to think about it while I'm sleeping."

With that, he carefully folds his treasured newspaper article, places it under his pillow, and goes to sleep.

In the morning, Fats is his old perky self once again. He devours a hearty breakfast of corn muffin crumbs topped off with a dab of jelly donut. He recites to us, from memory, the entire newspaper article. He even treats us to a little song.

"A jewel and a marvel, that's me, hee-hee!" he sings.

Then he is ready to start work on Number 6.

Before he begins, however, Fats makes a startling announcement. "This one is going to be different," he tells us. "I am going to create a collage with no food in it."

It is my turn to be shocked.

"You can't do it," I say.

"Yes, I can," he insists.

"No candy wrappers?" I will believe that when I see it.

"No candy, ice cream, gum, potato chip, pretzel, or corn chip wrappers," he promises.

Raymond and I are both speechless.

"Well," says Raymond finally. "Good luck."

Fats looks brave and determined. "It will be hard," he admits, "but we extremely talented artists like to do hard things."

Without food, Fats has no materials on hand. So before the Museum Cafe opens, he goes on a scouting mission. A few minutes later he returns, carrying a cough drop box, a bottle cap, and a subway token.

"That's a start," he says, looking pleased with himself.

"You can't use the cough drop box," I tell him.

"Why not?"

"Food," I answer.

"The bottle cap is kind of food too," Raymond points out.

Fats looks at the subway token. "Hmmm. What could I make out of one subway token?"

"I have another one in my junk corner," Raymond says. "And some other stuff you might be able to use. Come and look."

In the short time we've been living in the museum, Raymond has managed to collect an amazing amount of junk. To him, of course, it isn't junk at all. "Useful objects" is what he calls it. He has old envelopes of assorted sizes, three keys, two postage stamps, several safety pins, a hair clip, a *Visitor's Guide to New York City,* a knitting needle, a lipstick, a little mirror, a shoelace, an address book, two pencil stubs, and a credit card.

"Hmmm." Fats studies Raymond's junk for a long time. He picks up things, looks at them, then puts them down again.

"Well, what do you think?" asks Raymond.

"I don't know." Fats shakes his head. "I just don't feel inspired. You know, we extremely talented artists need to feel inspired in order to create."

"I know why you don't feel inspired," I tell him. "It's because none of this stuff is food."

Fats looks deeply hurt. "That isn't true, Marvin," he insists. "It's just—I don't know—I need more."

More. I can give him more. That's easy.

"If you want more, I know where to find it," I say. "There is more of everything in Central Park. What we need is a little collecting expedition."

Fats the Artist agrees. So does Raymond the World's Greatest Collector. And of course I, Marvin the Adventurer, like nothing better than a daring trip Outside. So that very afternoon we set off for Central Park.

"I think I know where we might be successful," says Raymond.

He has been studying his *Visitor's Guide to New York City,* so he now knows everything there is to know about the park. He leads us uphill and down and around and about, through a field of tall grass and a jungle of bushes, until we find ourselves face-to-face with an iron fence.

"There it is," he says.

Through the fence I see a children's playground.

"Oh, goody!" squeaks Fats.

I look where he is looking. I see what he sees. It is a little girl sitting on a bench, sucking on a lollipop.

"Fats," I say warningly. "Remember, no food."

"Uh—um—right," he agrees.

A bench made a satisfactory observation post and collecting station the last time we were in the park. So we slip through the bars of the fence and take up residence under the lollipop girl's bench.

We settle ourselves in some dry leaves. In case anyone looks under the bench, we will be safely hidden. Raymond unrolls his baby sock, ready to pack up all the treasures we will find. Meanwhile, I survey the action in this playground.

It is a busy, noisy place. The benches are crowded, filled with mothers and grandmothers, nurses and nannies, and, here and there, a father or two. Baby carriages and strollers are lined up next to the benches. Children are running around, sliding on slides, swinging on swings, riding on bikes. Not to mention playing in the sandbox right in front of us. They are laughing and shouting and arguing over toys.

I love a good commotion.

"This," I tell my gang, "is great."

Fats does not reply. I notice that he is still looking at the lollipop girl, gazing up through the slats in the bench. At that moment, she drops her lollipop stick. Immediately Fats grabs it and starts licking.

"Fats!"

"Just keeping my strength up," he tells me a little sheepishly. "You know, for all the collecting we have to do."

So far he hasn't done any collecting. But Raymond has. From the grass behind the bench he has retrieved a little plastic dinosaur and the remains of a bright pink balloon.

"Nice color!" says Fats.

In the next few minutes, Raymond adds a puzzle piece with a duck on it, a baby's pacifier, and three rather soggy baseball cards. And I find a couple of treasures: a sky-blue marble and a shiny black chess piece.

"It's the king!" Raymond exclaims. "Good work, Marvin."

"Oh, wow!" says Fats. "I get to have a king in my collage."

Fats himself still hasn't collected anything. He keeps looking up at the lollipop girl, who now has no lollipop.

"What are you doing?" I demand.

"Shhhh," he whispers. "I'm waiting. She's playing with her Barbie doll."

Sure enough, before long a little sock comes drifting down. Then a tiny diamond necklace. And a gold high-heeled shoe falls in his lap.

"I love it!" says Fats.

I have my eye on the lollipop girl's little brother. He has taken a whole fleet of miniature trucks into the sandbox. I see two dump trucks, an oil truck, a bulldozer, a cement mixer, and a fire truck. Now, these are real treasures. If only I could collect one for Fats.

I keep my sharp eyes glued on those trucks. But the boy does not drop, lose, or forget about any of them. In fact, he's not letting them out of his sight. When another boy tries to play with the fire truck, this one lets out a loud shriek.

"Mine!" he cries.

"Now, Jason." His mother jumps up and hurries to the sandbox. "You know we like to share our toys."

"No we don't!" the boy yells.

I can see I am not going to be collecting a truck from this kid.

So I turn my attention elsewhere, to the bench next to ours. And that is when I spot it. The best treasure of all. A treasure so wonderful, so exciting, so totally fabulous that I can't possibly give it to Fats. This one is all mine.

It is a bright red racing car.

I can hardly believe my eyes. There it is, alone and abandoned, sitting under the bench just waiting for me.

"I'll be back," I tell my gang.

On closer inspection, my racing car looks like it has been there awhile. It is dusty, and the red paint is chipped. Also, unlike the racing cars in Macy's toy department, it doesn't seem to have a battery. But I don't care.

I hop right in. I put my paws on the steering wheel. This car was made for me, I can feel it. I start my engine.

"*Vrr-rooom!*"

In my head I hear the purr of a powerful engine. And a moment later, the excited voice of the announcer, just like on TV. "They're off! It's the start of the New York City 500!"

Flags wave and people in the grandstands cheer as the race begins. My red car leaps forward, speeding down the straightaway. As we approach the first turn, my car and two others pull ahead of the rest of the field.

Going into the turn, I see a yellow car trying to pass me.

"Oh, no you don't!" I step on the accelerator.

My car responds beautifully. With a roar of my powerful engine, I leave the yellow car in the dust.

Now it is just the two of us, a black car and my red one. Again and again we circle the track. We are nose to nose, fender to fender. First I edge ahead, then the black car does.

"We'll see about that!" I call for more speed, and my car delivers.

It is the last lap. Still the black car stays next to me. Can my car hang on to win? Can I coax a last burst of speed from its trusty engine?

I press the accelerator to the floor.

My car surges forward. It inches ahead of the black car, just as we round the final turn. Seconds later I am across the finish line. First! The winner of the New York City 500! And I've set a new world speed record too! The fans in the grandstands cheer wildly as my car finally comes to a stop.

I step out to take a bow.

Just then my wonderful daydream is interrupted as I notice something out of the corner of my eye. Fats. He is standing out in the open in front of our bench. What can he be thinking of?

I see what he is thinking of. Popcorn. A boy in a blue baseball hat is riding in circles on his bike, nibbling on popcorn. And dropping popcorn.

As I watch, Fats grabs a piece and runs back under the bench.

"Okay, Fats," I mumble. "You had your fun."

But one piece of popcorn—or anything else that's edible—is never enough for Fats.

The boy drops another piece. Fats runs out again.

He has never been swift like me, able to dart from place to place faster than the human eye can see. Surely someone will notice him. I hold my breath.

All the mothers and grandmothers, nurses and nannies, and a father or two are busy watching their children. No one seems to see a fat mouse snatching up popcorn right in front of their noses.

I let out a sigh of relief.

And send Fats my most powerful thought-wave. "No more popcorn. Not a kernel. Not a crumb. None."

For a moment I think he has received my message. Then the boy on the bike hits a bump and drops a whole handful of popcorn.

Fats has to have it.

"Fats!" I hiss. I wave at him to go back. But when Fats is thinking about food, he can't see or hear anything else.

So he doesn't notice that this big popcorn giveaway has attracted the attention of another park animal. And one I'm not particularly fond of. A pigeon.

Pigeons, as everyone knows, love to eat. They are as greedy as any mouse of hearty appetite. And like any mouse of hearty appetite, they aren't too fussy about what they eat. However, unlike us mice, who are known for our easygoing nature, pigeons have bad dispositions. To put it bluntly, they are mean and nasty creatures.

Fats does not want to get into an altercation with a pigeon.

He pays no attention to it. All he sees right now is popcorn. He is gathering it up and gobbling it down as fast as his paws and jaws will go.

"Fats!" I say, louder this time. "Watch out!"

Again he doesn't hear me. So he is totally surprised when he and the pigeon grab the same piece of popcorn at the same time.

"Hey!" protests Fats indignantly. "Let go!"

The pigeon does not let go. It has the popcorn firmly in its beak. It is a rather plump pigeon, I see. And much bigger than Fats.

Fats doesn't care about that. "It's mine!" he cries.

He glares at the pigeon. He tugs and pulls and stamps his feet.

The pigeon will not budge. It ruffles its feathers. It flaps its wings.

It is an epic struggle. Greed against greed. Fat mouse against fat pigeon. And all for a little piece of popcorn.

Suddenly someone notices.

"Look at that!" cries the boy on the bike.

Then everyone else on the benches does.

"Oh, my goodness!" cries a mother.

"It's a mouse!" cries a nanny.

"Are you sure?" asks a father. "Maybe it's a rat."

They jump up and grab their children, plopping them into strollers and wheeling them away.

"Oh, goody!" exclaims the lollipop girl. "I love mice!"

"Courtney!" says her mother. "Don't touch it!" But before she can stop her, the lollipop girl reaches for Fats.

That is when I spring into action. Faster than a speeding racing car, I zip out from my hiding place. I grab Fats by the tail, then dart under our bench. Raymond is ready, his baby sock tied up and slung over his shoulder. In seconds, we have ducked out the back way and are running for our lives.

The lollipop girl comes running after us.

"Come back, little mouse!" she calls.

Her mother runs after her.

"Come back here, Courtney!" she calls.

The boy who started all the trouble with that free popcorn runs after her. And his nanny. And a policeman. A policeman? Is he going to arrest Fats for stealing popcorn?

But none of them have a chance against me. I am speedy. I am slick. I am slippery. Also, I know we can fit between the bars of that iron fence and humans can't.

It doesn't take long to lose them. In no time we are out of that playground. We race through the tall grass and into a tangled jungle of bushes where no one can spot us. I want to keep going just to make sure, but Fats suddenly flops down, panting and puffing.

"I can't go a step farther," he wheezes.

We rest comfortably under a bush for a few minutes. Then I notice that I'm not really resting so comfortably. Something sharp is poking my elbow.

I dig around in the dirt, and unearth a toy soldier.

Wiping it off, I present it to Fats.

"A toy soldier! Wow! This is perfect. Thanks, Marvin," he says.

I have to admit it is the best find of the day. Except, of course, for my racing car.

Fats is so excited, he jumps to his feet.

"Let's go!" he says. "I can't wait to get started on Number Six."

12

I Make Fats
Even More Famous

Fats gets right to work, using all the terrific materials we collected in Central Park. The little dinosaur, the marble, the chess piece, the pacifier, Barbie clothes, car parts, and a few other things Raymond picked up while I wasn't looking. Like two dominoes and a rocket ship. And, of course, my wonderful toy soldier. And astonishingly enough, Fats creates a collage without a single food ingredient.

I can hardly believe my eyes. Then I notice the pacifier.

"That is usually found in a baby's mouth," I point out. "Does that count?"

Raymond considers the matter. "It does go into the mouth," he answers. "Still, it could hardly be called food. No, I think a pacifier is all right."

"Well, then," I say. "Congratulations, Fats. They—uh, we—said it couldn't be done, but you did it. An impressive achievement."

Fats looks modestly at the floor. "It was hard," he admits. "Probably the hardest thing I have ever done. But I did it for Art."

We all agree that Number 6 is Fats's finest work yet. And all because of my stupendous find, the toy soldier.

"Doesn't the toy soldier just set off the the rest of the collage with its vibrant green color?" I say.

Raymond nods thoughtfully. "And the juxtaposition of the modern soldier next to the ancient dinosaur is brilliant. Just brilliant."

Fats is delighted with the comments of his two art critics. "Thank you," he says with a little bow. "You are very kind."

"That toy soldier just *makes* Number Six," I continue.

But Fats no longer seems to be listening. His eyes have a faraway look.

"Ssshhh," whispers Raymond. "The artist is thinking."

The artist sits in his thinking pose, chin resting on paws, for a long time. Then he wanders over to Raymond's junk corner. He retrieves the three baseball cards that Raymond brought back from the park and has been drying out. He arranges and rearranges them on the floor.

"I think he is thinking about Number Seven," I whisper.

Fats arranges the cards again. He sighs. And finally he speaks.

"I have a vision," he says in a dreamy voice. "For Number Seven."

I knew it.

"But I don't have enough."

"Enough what?" I ask.

"Baseball stuff."

My first thought is that we will have to make another trip to Central Park. But Raymond, who looks like he hasn't recovered from our last one, doesn't agree.

"It is baseball season," he reminds us. "Lots of kids come to the museum with their parents. And kids are always dropping things. So we're bound to collect some good baseball materials right here."

It turns out Raymond is correct. That very night we find a copy of *Sports Weekly* under a table. Fats sets right to work ripping it up. The next night I come upon a crumpled baseball card under the radiator. Fats sits on it to straighten it out. Raymond finds another one the following night. And I come up with another exciting find: two tickets to a Mets game.

"How could anyone drop these?" I wonder. "Now they can't go to the game."

Raymond shows me that the tickets are

ripped. "They already went to the game," he says. "Those are just ticket stubs."

Fats makes another great find in his favorite place, the trash can.

It is a key chain. The chain part is broken, which must be why it is in the trash. But attached to it is a miniature baseball player, dressed in a complete uniform and red cap and carrying a tiny bat.

Raymond examines it.

"It must have belonged to a tourist," he decides.

"Why?" I ask.

"Because this isn't a Met or a Yankee," he explains. "He is wearing a Red Sox uniform."

Fats is thrilled with his discovery, even if his baseball player isn't from a New York team. He looks over his growing pile of baseball stuff.

"I think I have enough now," he says.

Fats begins work on Number 7 the next morning. He arranges and rearranges all his materials until he has just the arrangement he is looking for. Then he starts cutting and pasting. Raymond stands by to assist him. I exercise my jaw on a tough crust of pumpernickel bagel, while keeping a watchful eye on what is happening in the Museum Cafe.

Not much is going on at the moment. It is a quiet morning, somewhere between breakfast and lunch. A couple of ladies are having tea and muffins at one table. A man is doing a crossword puzzle at another. Ever on the alert for baseball materials, I check out both tables carefully. But none of these customers are wearing or carrying anything interesting.

The cafe is so quiet that the workers have time to talk to each other.

"So," says the cashier. "Who do you think the mystery artist is? Marco the cook or Sophie the ticket-seller?"

My ears instantly perk up.

The woman behind the serving counter laughs. "Personally, Doris, I think it must be Stanley, the guy who sweeps up. You know, his mind is never on his work."

Stanley, the guy who sweeps up. My lightning-fast brain makes an instant connection. They are talking

about none other than our
friend, the careless sweeper.

Doris laughs. "That's a
good one, Maria. Well,
you never know. Stranger
things have happened."

That's a good one, all
right. Stanley the Careless
Sweeper, indeed. It's a good
thing Fats isn't listening. He would be insulted.

I am just beginning to feel insulted on Fats's
behalf when I notice something that makes me
forget all about silly sweepers. A group of mothers and children have just settled in at the corner
table. There are two mothers and about six children of assorted ages, from babies to middle-size
ones. They are creating a lot of fuss, arguing and
changing seats and talking about what they don't
want for lunch. But what catches my eye is the
baby sitting in a stroller next to the table.

He is dressed entirely in Yankee clothing.

He has on a Yankee shirt and Yankee overalls and a little blue Yankee jacket. On his head
is a Yankee cap. And sitting in the stroller next
to him is a stuffed bear also wearing a Yankee
shirt.

Oh, wow! This is a treasure trove of baseball stuff. Fats will go crazy. I've got to get it for him.

But how? I can't undress this baby in the middle of the Museum Cafe.

I remain calm. I put my powerful laser-like brain to work on the problem.

Hmmm. I could kidnap the baby. Tie him up, take his clothes, then return him, safe and sound, to his anxious parents. His anxious, grateful parents. Who might even give me a reward. A very generous reward. But no, I decide regretfully. That would take too long. Fats is already at work on Number 7.

I could follow the baby. Out of the cafe, out of the museum, to wherever he lives. I wait for his mother to undress him and put him to bed. Then, quicker than you can say "New York Yankees," I steal his clothes and run back here.

A little tricky but do-able, I'm thinking, when I observe something else.

The baby has taken off his Yankee hat. As I watch, he throws it on the floor. Then he laughs.

His mother, still talking to the other mother, picks up the hat, brushes it off, and puts it back on his head.

But it doesn't stay there. Again the baby throws the Yankee hat on the floor. Again he laughs, like this is a big joke.

This time a girl who seems to be his sister picks it up.

"Stop that, Mikey," she says.

But Mikey doesn't stop. This must be his favorite game. Over and over, he throws the Yankee hat on the floor. Over and over, his sister picks it up.

Aha! says my powerful laser-like brain. I may not be able to get Fats a complete Yankee outfit, but I bet I can get him a baby-size Yankee hat.

I charge into action. Darting out from our cupboard, I weave my way between table and chair legs until I reach the table in the corner. I pause alertly, aware of the danger from all those feet beneath it. However, I am safer than I expected. Most of them don't touch the floor. I am also just in time for a full-course lunch. These kids are dropping everything: potato chips, bits of bacon, a whole slice of rye bread, cheese. Even half a pickle, one of Fats's favorites. If I were Fats, I could forget all about my mission.

However, I am not distracted. I help myself to

a chip and a few bites of cheese. I love Swiss, but why does it have all those empty holes? Then I position myself near the baby's stroller. And I wait.

Three more times this laughing baby throws his Yankee hat on the floor. Three more times his patient sister picks it up.

But the fourth time she doesn't. She is too busy eating a chocolate chip cookie.

Mikey has forgotten the game too. He is too busy looking at the cookie.

The Yankee hat is all mine.

I grab it and run. That is when I notice that the Museum Cafe is no longer quiet. While I have been acquiring my prize, people have been coming in. Most of the tables are filled, and the spaces in between are crowded with heavy, sharp-heeled, moving feet. It is the worst time of day in the Museum Cafe. Lunchtime.

How can I get this treasure back to Fats? I ask my powerful laser-like brain. And it answers right away. Use a disguise.

Of course. This is what Raymond always recommends. And I am holding on to the perfect disguise. The Yankee hat itself.

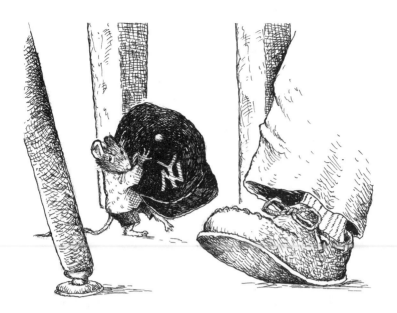

Concealing myself beneath the hat, I begin a long, slow journey across the floor. I stick close to the wall, making my way around shopping bags, purses, packages, and feet, moving an inch at a time. If anyone looks down, all they will see is a crumpled, dusty, dark-blue baseball hat. I am hoping no Yankee fan happens to look down.

It is an excruciatingly slow trip. Especially for a mouse who loves speed. But at the end of it, I am able to put my fast feet to work. For the last few yards, I have nowhere to hide. No chairs or tables or dark shadows. It is open floor. I take a deep breath. Then, with an incredible burst of speed, I dash across that dangerous no-man's-land.

Still hidden under the hat, I announce my arrival.

"Hi, gang," I say.

No one answers. I peek out. Raymond and Fats are so busy gluing, they probably didn't even notice I was gone.

I tiptoe closer. "Ahem!"

"What is that?" I hear Fats ask.

"Why, it looks like a baseball hat," says Raymond.

"Ta-da!" I say, stepping out with a flourish. "This isn't just any old baseball hat. It is a real, genuine New York Yankee hat. Just a little something I picked up in my travels."

"A Yankee hat?" Fats squeals. "Oh boy, I know just where to put it!"

I knew he would like it.

"Oh, and Fats," I say. "In case you're hungry, I brought you a little snack."

I present him with half a pickle.

"A Yankee hat and a pickle!" Fats chortles, beside himself with glee. "All in one day. This is too much. I mean, it's just right. I mean, Marvin, you're the best!"

I take a little bow.

"I know it," I say.

With the Yankee hat and the pickle for inspiration, Fats works feverishly on Number 7. And by closing time, he is ready for another installation.

Thanks to the careless sweeper, we have no trouble slipping out of the cafe with Numbers 6 and 7. Carefully we carry Fats's latest, greatest work to his personal display area.

"Fantastic," I say.

"Outstanding," says Raymond.

"I wonder what those art critic people will say," says Fats.

Those art critic people are excited. Not to mention enthusiastic, ecstatic, and thrilled. We find that out the next day as they and the museum visitors crowd around Numbers 6 and 7. The crowds have grown so big, in fact, that the ticket-taker now allows only a few people at a time into Fats's exhibit area. We hear them buzzing about color and pattern and all that other art-critic stuff. And the day after that, Raymond reads all about it in the newspaper.

"Listen to this," he says, putting on his spectacles.

"The latest works by an unknown artist to appear at the Guggenheim Museum are as intriguing as the earlier ones, according to its director, Marguerite Devereux. 'These miniature collages have such remarkable detail,' she told this reporter, 'that they seem to have been put together by tiny hands.'"

Fats and I have to smile at that.

"Does she say anything about the Yankee hat?" I ask.

Raymond shakes his head. "No, just the usual remarks about the amazing use of color, wonderful sense of design, and unusual choice of found objects. Oh, and the comments about society."

"What did I say about society?" Fats wants to know.

"Well, all the critics seem to agree," Raymond tells him. "Number Six speaks about the child-centered nature of our society. And Number Seven is about the sports-obsessed nature of our society."

Fats thinks it over carefully. He nods.

"That's what I thought I was saying," he says.

Raymond keeps reading.

"Oh, my," he exclaims suddenly. "Listen to this. *According to Ms. Devereux, the museum plans to give the mystery artist a one-man (or one-woman) show*

in a special small gallery in late May. 'We are hopeful,'
she said, 'that the artist will come forward to reveal his
or her identity at that time.'"

"A one-mouse show!" I say. I can't believe it.

Neither can Fats. He is pinching himself to
make sure he is awake. He is skipping and dancing and cartwheeling around.

"A one-mouse show!" he crows. "Hip, hip,
hooray!"

Finally he subsides in a breathless heap. "Who
would have thought it?" he says in wonderment.
"Me, a poor mouse from a large family, brought
up in the dark, damp basement of a shoe repair
shop on the Lower East Side. A mouse with no
paints, no canvas, no art supplies of any kind.
And barely even enough to eat. I struggled. I
lived on scraps from trash cans and crumbs from
candy machines. I was forced to use mustard and
mayonnaise and ketchup for paint. And now this!
My own one-mouse show at the Googlestein!"

"Guggenheim," corrects Raymond.

"Exactly," says Fats.

13

I Prepare for My Finest Hour

With his one-mouse show only days away, Fats goes into a frenzy of creative activity.

"Number Eight is going to be my finest work yet," he proclaims. "It will be a comment on all of society."

For several nights he scurries about, scavenging all sorts of found objects with the help of his assistant, Raymond the Collector. They not only scour the Museum Cafe, but the kitchen as well. And the trash cans, counters, phone booths, benches, and lost-and-found department of the museum itself.

They come back with some interesting objects. A pair of sunglasses. A potato peeler. A car key. A gold ring. Cinnamon sticks. Tickets to the opera. A parking ticket. A mousetrap.

We stare in horror at this instrument of torture.

"I can't look," mumbles Fats, covering his eyes. "It's too awful."

But I can. Not only can I look at that mousetrap, I can jump up and down on it until it crumbles into a pile of sawdust and wire.

Raymond stops me. "Wait a minute, Marvin," he says. "This mousetrap is also a comment on all of society. I think Fats should include it in his masterpiece."

Pulling himself together, Fats reluctantly agrees. "As long as it won't catch me while I'm gluing it on."

Raymond assures him that the mousetrap is not set. And he presents Fats with a special gift: the torn cover from a crossword puzzle book.

"It's to glue everything onto," he explains. "A comment on all of society needs to be bigger than an envelope."

Fats is delighted to work in a larger size. He gets started right away, happily humming to himself while he sorts and arranges his large selection of found objects.

While Fats is creating his finest work yet, my thoughts turn to my own finest hour. This, of course, is my plan to turn the railing on the last curve of the museum's long ramp into a ski jump. I have studied the railing carefully, and I see two possible problems. One is its narrow and possibly slippery surface. I could fall off and break all my bones. I am not too concerned about this. A mouse of my exceptional skill and balance should not have any real difficulties. But I have to admit I'm a little worried about the bottom. That is because, unlike the ski jumpers on TV, I won't be jumping onto a nice, soft, snowy slope. I'll be jumping onto flat, hard stone.

I am a tough guy. I can take it. However, I also remember my painful collision with a hard glass door. There must be an easier way.

I ponder the problem while I listen to Fats doing his own pondering. "The subway token next to the ring? No. Maybe next to the bottle cap? No. Oh, dear, it has to be perfect."

No solutions for my problem pop immediately into my agile brain.

Raymond the Big Thinker loves to solve

problems. Back in the days when we lived in a movie theater, he read as many issues of *Popular Mechanics* and *Science Today* as he could get his paws on.

"Raymond, old boy," I begin, and I describe to him the little difficulty of my ski jump onto stone.

I wait for Raymond's solution. But he doesn't answer.

"Well?" I say impatiently. Then I notice that he can't answer. He is too busy chewing. His cheeks are puffed out like Fats's on his last birthday, when he gulped down an entire cupcake.

"What's the matter with you?" I demand.

Raymond opens his mouth. Out comes a small pink bubble. It grows until it is bigger than his nose. Bigger than his head. Almost as big as his entire body.

"Stop!" I order.

Suddenly the bubble bursts. Raymond reappears, strands of pink gum dangling from his ears and tangled in his whiskers.

"Sorry, Marvin," he says, calmly wadding up the gum. "I was just preparing some glue for Number Eight. I found two whole pieces of Dubble Bubble under that table where the Yankee baby was sitting. Now, what is the problem again?"

I explain once more about the tiny inconvenience of landing at top speed on a stone floor.

"I see." Raymond shakes his head. "We can't have that. Well, I'm sure we can come up with a solution. However, this will require careful scientific study. The first thing we need to do is take a few measurements. And after that I will make some calculations."

He goes into his junk corner, which, thanks to Fats, is no longer piled quite so high. He rummages around until he comes up with a little ruler, a pencil stub, and an old envelope.

"All right, Marvin," he says. "Let's go look at this railing."

We leave Fats still arranging his objects. "The texture of the tea bag next to the sunglasses makes an interesting contrast," he mutters to himself. "Then there is the square shape next to the round. Yes, all in all, a pleasing combination, I think."

I lead Raymond under the door and down the hall to the trouble spot at the bottom of the railing.

"Hmmm. I see what you mean," he says.

Raymond paces around, viewing the situation

from all angles. He takes out his ruler and measures the height of the railing where it ends. He writes some numbers on the envelope. Then he walks up the ramp, counting his steps and jotting down more numbers. Returning to the bottom, he makes himself comfortable on the ledge of the pool.

"I'll probably be going—oh—around a hundred miles an hour," I offer, trying to be helpful.

"Mmm. Yes, I'm sure you will," mumbles Raymond.

His pencil flies over the paper as he calculates furiously. He frowns down at his numbers. "That can't be right. Did I forget the acceleration of gravity?" He erases just as furiously.

I wait patiently, looking for pennies in the pool, while Raymond draws little diagrams with arrows going this way and that, and mutters to himself something about potential and kinetic energy. He calculates like crazy some more. And erases some more.

I spot two pennies. I am just thinking about diving in to retrieve them when Raymond announces, "I've got it!"

He goes over to where the railing ends, then walks away, carefully counting out his steps.

"Here," he says, marking a little X on the floor. "Here is where we will place your pillow."

My pillow. Of course! I knew all along that's what I needed for a soft landing. A pillow, placed on the X, will solve all my problems.

But where am I going to get a pillow?

While Raymond goes over his calculations one more time to make sure his X is at the precisely correct spot, I turn my attention to the pillow problem. When and where was the last time I saw a pillow? I strain my brain trying to remember. Raymond does not have one in his junk collection, I'm sure of that. And I can't recall seeing any pillows in the Museum Cafe. Or even during our excursions to Central Park.

No pillows in Raymond's collections. No pillows in the cafe. No pillows in the park.

Macy's! That is the last place I have seen a pil-

low. Or, to be more exact, hundreds of pillows. All piled high in the bedding department. If we were in the toy department right now, those pillows would be just an escalator ride away. Not only that, but I would have my choice of all different shapes and sizes. Fat or skinny. Giant size or baby size. Firm, soft, or super-soft. I think for this occasion, super-soft might be the best choice.

I will have to go to Macy's and bring back a pillow. It won't be easy. Pillows are bulky. They are heavy. They are a bit awkward for a mouse to carry. And how am I going to get one through Macy's bothersome revolving door?

I'll find a way. I can't let a little obstacle like a revolving door stand in the way of my finest hour.

"Raymond," I say. "It's time for a little trip to Macy's."

Raymond puts down his pencil. "Macy's?" he says, looking puzzled. "What for?"

"To raid the pillow department," I explain.

Raymond gazes at me for a long moment. "I see. Actually, Marvin, I don't think that will be necessary."

"It won't?"

"No. Come with me."

I follow as he jumps down from the pool ledge

and scurries across the floor. He heads directly for the Information counter, where a little lady with white hair sits every day handing out museum brochures. He stops next to her chair and points.

"There," he says, "is your pillow."

I look up. Sure enough, this museum worker has made herself comfortable in her chair. She has installed a yellow flowered pillow with ruffles around the edges to sit on.

"Perfect!"

I zip right up to try it out.

I wouldn't exactly call it super-soft. It might even be considered firm. But I feel sure it will do.

"Raymond," I say, "I am ready for perhaps the most daring, dangerous, death-defying exploit of my career. I am ready to Rollerblade down the railing and go flying through the air."

14

I Rescue Fats
From Himself

As it turns out, my daring, dangerous, death-defying exploit on the railing doesn't take place that night. Or the next night either. That is because of Fats and his finest work of art yet, Number 8.

He works on it nonstop, without sleeping, without pausing for a bite of coconut donut for breakfast or peanut butter pecan chocolate chip brownie for lunch. And when I offer him half a pretzel for dinner, Fats refuses.

"I don't have time for eating," he tells me, without even looking up from his gluing.

I am amazed. I never thought I would hear

those words coming out of his mouth. This is a brand-new Fats. A mouse of hard work. A mouse of dedication to his Art. A mouse who, if this keeps up, will not even be Fats anymore. We may have to start calling him Slim.

In less than twenty-four hours, Number 8 is finished and ready to hang. Raymond and I stand back to look at it.

Number 8 is Fats's largest work so far. It is crowded with all kinds of stuff, from postcards to baseball cards to credit cards. From Barbie clothes to baby rattles. From buttons to subway tokens to a gold ring. From toy car wheels to real car keys. From lipsticks to toothpicks to lollipop sticks. Yes, Fats has managed to sneak in a few food objects too. I spot a Tootsie Roll wrapper in one corner and a chocolate chip next to the ring.

"Is it my finest work yet?" asks Fats anxiously.

"Absolutely," answers Raymond.

"Positively," I echo. "And vibrant too."

"What do you think it says about society?" Fats wants to know.

"Hmmm." Raymond gives the question his most careful consideration. He walks up and down, peering at Number 8 from all angles. He gives his whiskers a good twirl. "Well, Fats," he begins.

And he goes into a long lecture about the popular culture of today, consumer spending, the environment, and the clash of old and new values. I don't understand a word he's saying.

"Not only that," I add when Raymond finally stops talking. "It says society is full of stuff."

"Right!" Fats grins happily.

We hang his masterpiece that night. And when the museum opens the next morning, we discover that the critics agree. Number 8 is the mystery artist's finest work yet.

"Brilliant!" "Perceptive!" "Acutely observant!" "Right on the money!" Those are some of the exclamations we hear from the Very Important People who crowd around Fats's exhibit. More critics and museum directors and reporters and photographers come to see his new collage than ever before. Reporters are interviewing everyone in sight. Flashbulbs are going off every few seconds. People are pushing and shoving, trying to get closer to Number 8.

Up in our planter, Fats's face wears a nonstop grin.

"Oh, wow!" he says, going into his bouncing-ball routine. "I think they like it!"

They like it so much, it seems like the com-

motion will never end. By the middle of the morning, I am tired of all the ooh-ing and ahh-ing. I am tired of fancy words like "exhilarating" and "illuminating." I am tired of hearing the word "genius" over and over. And they aren't even talking about me.

"Let's go have a snack," I tell my gang.

Fats doesn't hear me. He is in another world, a beautiful world of smiles and applause, listening to the Very Important People praise Number 8.

"I said snack," I repeat, louder. "As in coconut donut. As in pickle. As in CHEESE!"

I have Fats's attention now.

"Now that you mention it, I think I forgot to eat. I'm a little hungry." He pats his stomach. He drools. Now he is beginning to look like the old Fats. "In fact, I'm starving."

"Let's go," I say.

With everyone's eyes on Number 8, we have no trouble climbing down from our planter and stealing through the shadows to the Museum Cafe. In no time at all, Fats is feasting on yesterday's leftovers.

He eats as if his last meal was a month ago. When he finally finishes his last bite of lemon tart, he licks the crumbs off his whiskers and asks, "Didn't I hear you mention cheese?"

"Well, yes," I admit. "But that was just to wake you up. We don't actually have any right now."

"Phooey." Fats looks disappointed. Also stuffed. Patting his expanded stomach, he retreats to his coffee-cup bed for a nap.

His nap lasts about two minutes. Even in the Museum Cafe, there is no peace today.

The first thing I notice is raised voices. Looking out, I see a bunch of feet milling around. On closer inspection, I notice that the owners of the feet are not carrying food trays. They are carrying notebooks, tape recorders, and cameras. And I recognize the same reporters and photographers who were crowded around Number 8 a little while ago.

"What's going on?" asks Fats, creeping out of his coffee cup.

"Just some more commotion," I tell him.

"The cafe workers are being interviewed," says Raymond. "And it sounds like it's about the mystery artist."

I see Doris, the talkative cashier, in the middle

of a group of reporters. She seems to be enjoying their attention.

"There has been speculation," one reporter is saying, "that the mystery artist might be some-one who works here in the cafe, since so many of the collages have a food theme. How do you feel about that?"

"I have to say," answers Doris in a loud voice, "that I agree. In fact, I have my own suspicions about who it might be."

"Who is that?" asks the reporter.

"Well," says Doris, "the young man who sweeps up at night—Stanley is his name—wears strange clothes. You know, torn jeans and sloppy shirts. He just looks like an artist to me. And he never has his mind on his work. And do you know what else?" She lowers her voice so we have to strain our ears to hear. "He wears an earring."

"No kidding," says another reporter. "Where is this Stanley? Can we talk to him?"

"Today is his day off," Doris replies. "But come back tomorrow. You'll see. I bet he's the one."

There is more milling around, more questions, more flashbulbs as Doris happily poses for pictures. Then, little by little, things quiet down as the reporters and photographers leave and the cafe workers go back to work.

Fats is in a state of shock. "Did she say what I think she said?" he mumbles. "Our sweeper, the one who leaves us all that nice food, is the mystery artist? And his name is Stanley?"

"No, no," I correct him. "His name is Stanley. But he isn't the mystery artist. You are."

"I know that." Fats is indignant. "But no one else does. So, what if this Stanley steps forward on opening night and tells everyone he is the mystery artist. He will be famous and I won't."

"Now, Fats," Raymond says soothingly. "Don't get excited. That's not going to happen."

Fats isn't listening. "I won't have it," he mutters to himself. "No sir, not this time. After all my struggles. Growing up without a penny to my name for paints. Living on stale crusts of bread and once in a while a crumb of coconut donut. It's not fair!"

"We know," I reassure him.

"I have to take a stand," Fats babbles on, his whiskers quivering, "for all mouse-kind. We mice never get credit for our achievements. But

I'm going to change that. I will step forward on opening night and tell everyone I am the mystery artist. And then," he finishes with a little smile, "I'll be famous."

I stare at him. Fats has never made such a long speech in his life. And he never cared about mouse-kind before. What has gotten into him?

"No, Fats," says Raymond quietly. "You can't do it."

"You *won't* do it!" I order loudly.

"But I have to," answers Fats.

Raymond and I attempt to reason with him. We review all the many dangers of being noticed by humans. We remind him of our narrow escape just days ago after his fight with the pigeon in Central Park.

Fats shakes his head. "I don't care," he insists.

"Exterminator," I say to him. "Exterminator, EXTERMINATOR, **EXTERMINATOR!**"

Fats gulps. "I don't care," he quavers.

Raymond tries a different argument. "Being famous isn't always so wonderful," he points out. "In fact, it can be a nuisance. If you are famous, people are always looking at you and following you and taking your picture. And asking a million questions. Really, it's tiring."

"It doesn't sound so bad to me." Fats is smiling again.

"You will lose your freedom," Raymond warns. "You will lose your time. Pretty soon you will find you can't even do your art."

Fats gives that a moment's thought.

"I don't care," he whispers.

And he walks away.

"Where are you going?" I demand.

"To look at the doll clothes in Raymond's junk corner," Fats replies. "If I'm going to be famous, I need something to wear."

By the next morning, Fats has put together a nice little artist's outfit. It consists of faded overalls, a too-big white shirt, and a funny little hat.

"Do I look like an artist?" he asks.

"You look like a clown," I tell him.

Fats's feelings are obviously hurt.

"You look exactly the way an artist should look," Raymond assures him.

"I have to look good for my pictures." Fats parades in front of the cracked mirror in Raymond's junk corner. "They'll be taking a lot of pictures at the opening. And I'll be in the newspaper too. Maybe on the front page. Do you think

I might be on TV? Oh, dear, I'd better comb my whiskers."

While Fats is admiring himself, I notice that the noise level outside has been slowly rising. Peering out, I see the familiar feet of the reporters and photographers.

"They're back!" I announce.

Not only are they back, but they have multiplied since yesterday. With bigger cameras and brighter lights. And wires running all over the place. Fats was right. Some of those cameras are TV cameras.

"Over here!" calls Doris.

She is having the time of her life, posing for pictures and giving interviews. "Stanley should be here any minute," she tells a reporter. "You just ask him flat out if he's the mystery artist."

I don't see Stanley walk in. Too many feet and cameras and wires are in the way. But I know when he does. Suddenly all the feet are surging toward the door. Lights are flashing and voices are shouting.

"Are you Stanley?"

"May we ask you some questions?"

"Is it true, sir, that you are the mystery artist?"

We are at the edge of our cupboard, straining

to see. But it's no use. The crowd has Stanley completely surrounded.

However, we hear Doris. "Come on, guys," she says loudly. "Step back and give him room to breathe."

And a moment later we hear Stanley.

"I don't know what you're talking about," he says.

The voices rise again.

"Did you do the collages?"

"You know, the art that keeps appearing on the museum wall."

This time we hear Stanley's answer loud and clear.

"Me?" he says. "I'm a musician, not an artist."

My gang and I look at each other.

"Nice guy, that Stanley," I remark. "I always said so."

Fats grins. "That's why he always leaves us so much nice food."

"He may not be much of a sweeper," adds Raymond. "But he's an honest man."

The reporters and photographers seem disappointed, but they don't give up. They still surround him, shouting more questions. Meanwhile, Doris takes aside a small group of reporters. "You might want to talk to Mario, our cook," she says. "Everyone says he's an artist with food."

With that, a bunch of people make a dash for the kitchen.

A minute later Fats's nose starts to twitch.

"Am I dreaming?" he wonders out loud. "Or do I smell what I think I smell. Oh, boy! I haven't tasted any in so long!"

"Any what?" I ask.

Now Fats is twitching all over. "Camembert!" he crows. "It just fell out of that photographer's bag. I have to have it!"

And before I can snatch his tail to stop him, he darts out into the crowd of running feet.

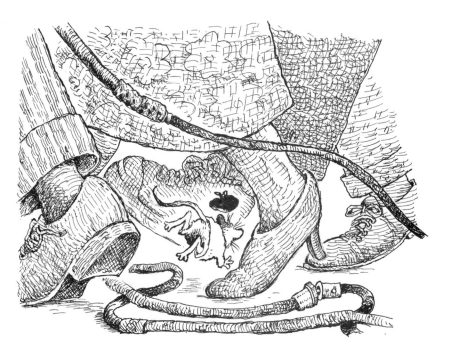

"Come back!" I order. But it is too late. Fats is gone.

Raymond peers after him in disbelief. "What were you thinking of, Fats?" he asks. "Oh, dear, this is terrible."

It is terrible, all right. Of all the foolhardy things Fats has ever done, this is the foolhardiest. In that throng of trampling feet, heavy cameras, and assorted sharp objects, he hasn't a chance of survival.

And it gets worse. A moment later, Mario the cook emerges from the kitchen. If there was commotion before, now it is pandemonium as the reporters and photographers push and shove and step on each other's toes, trying to get near him.

Raymond covers his eyes. "I can't look," he moans. "I'm afraid it's all over now. Poor Fats! To be trampled by the very people who admired his art."

"I told him so," I say.

"He was a true friend," Raymond goes on. Tears fill his eyes, fogging up his spectacles. "He may not always have been wise, but he had a kind heart. A cheerful disposition. A happy smile."

"An excellent stomach," I add.

"He was one of a kind," Raymond proclaims mournfully. "We shall never see his like again."

"That's for sure," I agree.

I'm beginning to feel a little teary-eyed my-self. My gang won't be the same without Fats. It will be smaller. We won't have so much food around. We won't have so many laughs either. And who will perform his famous cheese dance?

The noise outside goes on and on, but Raymond and I are no longer paying attention. We don't care what Mario the cook says or what the reporters and photographers do. We don't care who Doris decides is the real mystery artist. We know who he is. And he is gone forever.

After a while Raymond retires in dejection to his junk corner. I pace aimlessly up and down. I stop to peer inside Fats's coffee cup, where he spent so many happy hours napping. It is empty now, of course, except for a couple of old lollipop sticks and an empty jam pot.

One other thing about Fats: He sure was messy.

"Help!"

What was that? I ask myself. Probably noth-ing. Just some reporter being stepped on by some photographer.

"Help!" I hear it again.

That squeak sounds vaguely familiar. I back

out of Fats's coffee cup to see Fats himself crawling toward me.

He looks like he just came from a war zone. His face is squashed, as if he'd been run over by a tank. He is covered with dirt. His nice little artist's outfit is in tatters. And his tail has a strange-looking kink in it.

"What happened?" I ask.

"I don't know," groans Fats. "One minute I was reaching for the Camembert, and the next minute I was out cold. When I woke up, everyone was gone."

I listen. Sure enough, my sharp ears tell me that the cafe is quiet. Except for Doris. She is telling someone that now she's sure of it, the mystery artist has got to be Jimmy, the dishwasher.

"Fats!" cries Raymond joyfully. "You're alive! But you don't look so good."

"I don't feel so good," moans Fats.

He staggers to his coffee-cup bed and collapses.

For the next few hours, Fats sleeps. He wakes up, whimpering, "My head! My tail!" then goes back to sleep. Raymond and I wait on him hand and foot. Raymond places a toothpick splint on his broken tail. I bravely risk discovery by Doris to retrieve an ice cube for his aching head. And a

crumb of oatmeal cookie to keep his strength up.

It isn't until the next morning that Fats really wakes up. His eyelids flutter open and he looks right at me.

"I'm not going to do it, Marvin," he whispers.

"You're not going to do what?" I ask.

"Step forward," Fats answers. "Being famous is too dangerous."

15

I Attend a One-Mouse Show

It is opening night of Fats's one-mouse show—probably the very first one-mouse show ever. It is being held in his own small gallery on the second floor of the Googlestein Museum in New York City. And we, of course, are there.

We have been camped out behind a potted rose tree in the corner since early this morning, watching all the exhibit preparations unfold. First, we were treated to a lot of loud hammering and sawing, which didn't help Fats's still-aching head. A little later we saw Fats's artwork arrive, carried in by three assistants. Never had I seen humans handle anything so carefully. It was like they were carrying precious jewels. And they were all wearing white gloves.

"What is this white-glove thing?" I asked Raymond. In the movies it's the criminals who wear gloves, so as not to leave fingerprints.

"That's so they won't damage the art," Raymond informed me.

When he saw what was going on, Fats forgot all about his aches and pains. "That's my Number Three!" he whispered excitedly. "Oh, and look! Here comes Number Six!"

Shortly after that, a tall, thin, gray-haired man appeared. He looked kind of familiar. Where had I seen him before?

"Oh!" sighed Fats. "My favorite human in the whole world!"

Of course. This was the man we'd seen with the museum director when she first discovered Fats's art. The one who called Fats "very talented."

"He must be the curator of your exhibit," said Raymond.

"Curator?" I say.

"The man in charge of installing it," explains Raymond.

A long time went by while this curator guy debated with his assistants about where each piece of art should be hung. A great deal of measuring was done. Lights were moved. Artwork was moved. And moved again.

Number 3 was placed next to Number 5. The curator squinted his eyes, then slowly shook his head. Number 3 was moved next to Number 1. Number 8 was placed next to Number 4. The curator squinted, then frowned. Number 8 was moved to a special wall all by itself.

Finally Fats's favorite human stood back.

"Perfect," he decided, nodding with satisfaction. And he and his assistants went away.

For a little while then the gallery was quiet, and we were able to have our own private preview of Fats's one-mouse show.

We had to crane our necks to see it.

"He hung them too high," Fats complained.

"They're at human, not mouse, eye level," Raymond told him.

All in all, though, Fats was pleased.

"I did that?" he marveled, gazing up in admiration at Number 7.

"It's vibrant," I told him. "Especially the Yankee cap. Don't forget who got you that. And the Mets tickets. And the toy soldier on Number Six. And the chess piece. And—"

My list of important contributions was rudely interrupted by the arrival of a new set of workers, and we beat a hasty retreat to our rose tree. These workers carried in chairs and set up tables. They covered the tables with floor-length white table-cloths. They brought in trays of glasses and plates and cups.

Fats clapped his paws as he figured it out. "They're going to serve refreshments!" he announced.

He was even more delighted when he saw the platters that began to appear as the afternoon wore on, each one piled high with exotic-looking foods.

"And look!" he exclaimed. "They're mouse size!"

What, I asked myself, could be more fitting for Fats's one-mouse show than huge platters of bite-size food?

Now all the food is ready. Waiters are standing by. Soft music is playing from somewhere in the ceiling. Fats's favorite human, dressed in a fancy black suit and a bright red tie with purple squiggles, is standing near the door. And we have taken the opportunity during a quiet moment to install ourselves in a new observation post, concealed behind the tablecloth of the longest food table. A tiny rip in the cloth makes a perfect peephole.

The opening is about to open.

It starts quietly. A few people drift in and stand near the door, talking to the curator and each other. Then, a few minutes later, a few more. I recognize the museum director and some of the Very Important People we have seen before. They stand in small circles with glasses in their hands, talking and talking.

Fats is a little disappointed. "Stop talking," he mutters, "and look at the art."

More people arrive. The talking grows louder.

Finally, in groups of two and three and four, they begin to walk around, looking at the art on the walls. I see one small group in front of Number 7, waving their glasses as they talk.

"That's better," says Fats, relieved.

As time goes by, the room continues to fill up until it is crowded with people. Now the talking grows so loud, we can't hear the music anymore. We can't make out what anyone is saying about Fats's art. And we can't see anything through our peephole except wall-to-wall feet.

A lot of those feet are just inches from my nose as their owners help themselves to refreshments. Now, finally, we can hear what they are saying.

"Mmm, these little puff things look good."

"Do you know what they are?"

"No, but try one of the little sausage things. They're delicious."

Fats is disappointed again. "Stop talking about food," he grumbles, "and talk about art."

Just as he says those words, I see something fall past our peephole. Kind of a little puff thing.

Fats's nose twitches. His eyes open wide. His whiskers start to tremble. "Cheese!" he whispers.

I've been down this road before—just three

days ago, in fact. And I'm not going down it again. Like a true leader should, I am instantly on top of the situation. And on top of Fats.

"Stay right where you are," I order.

"Yes, Marvin," he whimpers. But his nose can't stop twitching and he keeps mumbling under his breath, "Oh wow! A puff made of cheese. And it's mouse size!"

"We'll get one later," I promise. "After the party is over."

Fortunately, our attention is distracted at that moment by the sound of a spoon tapping on glass. And then, over the buzz of talking, the voice of the curator.

"May I have everyone's attention, please?" he is saying.

Gradually the room quiets down, and he begins to speak.

"We are here tonight," he says, "to celebrate the opening of one of the most unusual and special exhibits in the history of the Guggenheim. It is unusual, as many of you know, because of the unexpected events that have occurred here during the past few weeks. These artworks have simply appeared, one by one, on our walls. They are unsigned, and no one to date has come forward to take credit for creating them. Though there has been much speculation about the artist's identity, he or she remains, as the newspapers have reported, a mystery artist."

He has Fats's full attention now.

"This is also a very special exhibit," the curator goes on, "because we are fortunate to be able to showcase an exciting new talent. I invite you to look carefully at the works of art hung on the walls of this gallery. Though their numbers are few and their size is small, their quality is remarkable. And what they have to say about our contemporary society is intriguing and provocative. I am sure you will agree with me that we are looking at the debut of an artist with a unique vision of the twenty-first century."

A murmur of agreement spreads through the crowd. A few people even begin to clap.

It's no wonder this is Fats's favorite human.

He is beaming like he just swallowed a whole platter of cheese puffs. "I'm exciting and remarkable and intriguing," he babbles. "Also provocative and unique. Uh—what is provocative?"

I have no idea. "I'm sure it's something good," I tell him.

"Shhhh," hisses Raymond.

The curator is still talking. "One final word," he says. "In the event that the mystery artist is in the room tonight, I would like to appeal to her or him to come forward. Please, whoever you are, let us show you our appreciation for these wonderful pieces of art."

There is a moment of silence as everyone waits to see if the mystery artist will come forward.

I look at the mystery artist. He looks at me.

"Don't even think about it," I warn, grasping him firmly by the ear.

"But they want me," he protests.

"No."

"They need me."

"Uh-uh."

"I could be famous."

"You could be dead. Look at your tail."

Fats stares down at his wounded tail. "Oh," he says. "Right."

"You don't need to be famous," Raymond tells him. "It's enough to have done your work and know it is good."

"And have a one-mouse show," I add.

Fats looks doubtful. I keep a good grip on his ear, just in case. Then he sighs loudly.

"I guess so," he agrees.

So the moment passes. The mystery artist does not come forward. And the party goes on.

And on. And on.

When everyone finally goes home, we have a party of our own. We feast on cheese puffs ("Yum! They melt in your mouth!" drools Fats) and little sausage things and lots of other delicacies that the party-goers dropped. A spinach this, a mushroom that. A spicy tidbit, a sweet-and-sour tidbit, and some so exotic, we can't figure out what they are. After we've stuffed ourselves full of refreshments, we take another tour of Fats's one-mouse show, taking turns saying, "Exciting! Remarkable! Intriguing! Provocative! Unique!"

At last we come to Number 8.

Fats gazes up at it for a long time. "Do you really think this is my finest work?" he asks.

"Absolutely," says Raymond.

"Positively," I say.

Fats studies it some more. Then he nods his head. "Yes," he says to himself. "I have to do it."

"Do what?" I ask.

But Fats ignores my question. "Do you have a pencil?" he asks Raymond.

Of course. Raymond always has everything.

Fats scurries up a chair until he can reach the

bottom of Number 8. He scribbles something in large letters, then comes down.

"I did it," he announces proudly. "I signed my name."

Raymond is staring up at Number 8. "Dudley?" he says.

"Dudley?" I echo.

"That is the name my mother gave me," Fats explains. "I wasn't always called Fats, you know."

I can't believe it. I have a gang member named Dudley.

"So," says Raymond, "the mystery artist isn't a mystery anymore."

"You came forward after all," I add.

"Yes," says Fats happily. "I did."

16

I Fly Through the Air
With the Greatest of Ease

After Fats's big triumph of last night, it is time to pack up and move back to our dollhouse home at Macy's. But before we can go, I have one more important thing to do. Finally my big moment has come. I am about to undertake the most daring, dangerous, death-defying exploit of my career. I am about to fly through the air off a ski jump.

Everything is in readiness. Raymond has calculated and recalculated the exact position of my landing pillow. He has measured and remeasured its placement. He has even added a woolly scarf left over from winter, which he found in the lost-and-found department, to assure me of a soft landing. And, in an act of supreme self-sacrifice, Fats has presented me with a bite of a Power Bar, which he found under Doris the cashier's chair.

"That's for quick energy," he says.

I am already brimming with energy. But I bolt down the Power Bar. Then I strap on my safety helmet and my Mickey Mouse knee guards. And something new that Raymond came up with after Fats's disastrous encounter with the reporters' and photographers' feet—a Daffy Duck tail guard. I sling my Rollerblades over my shoulder.

"Be careful, Marvin," warns Raymond the Worrier.

Careful, shmareful. What fun is that?

"Go fast and jump high!" cheers Fats.

That's better.

I walk up the ramp to the little landing where the railing begins. There I strap on my Rollerblades. I test out the wheels. I check once more to make sure all my safety equipment is in working order. Then I climb up on the railing.

For a moment I just stand there, looking down. I'm not nearly as high as I was when I skated all the way down from the top of the museum. But it feels high. Maybe that is because the railing is so narrow. It seems slippery too, beneath my wheels. It occurs to me that I could easily fall off before I reach the end of my runway. I might land on my valuable brain on the hard stone of the ramp. Or take a very high dive into the pool. And what about my landing pillow? Has Raymond really calculated its position correctly? Why does it look so small?

My knees are suddenly quivering like they are made of jelly. My heart is beating about a million times a minute, and my stomach doesn't feel so good either.

Maybe, I think, I don't really want to do this.

What? I can't believe I had that thought, even for an instant. I have been hanging out too long with Raymond the Worrier.

Snap out of it, I tell myself. This is me, Merciless Marvin the Magnificent. The Fearless. The Brave.

I remain perfectly still for a moment, until my heart slows down and my knees feel like I might be able to stand on them again. Then I straighten up. I wave to Raymond and Fats.

"I am ready," I call. "I am set. I am going.

"Right now!" I shout.

And I go.

I crouch down low over my Rollerblades, working up speed. That is how the ski jumpers do it on TV, I remember. Sure enough, I feel myself going faster and faster. I am hurtling through space at a hundred miles an hour, at least. And I am in perfect balance. I can't fall off.

I shoot down the runway. It seems like only seconds before I can see the bottom. It is coming up fast.

Get ready to jump, I tell myself.

Suddenly the railing ends. Just like a championship skier, I take a flying leap into space.

"Go, Marvin!" yells Fats.

"Remember the pillow!" cried Raymond.

I jump as high and far as I can. And for one glorious moment, I am flying. Soaring through the air with the greatest of ease. Like a bird. Like a plane. Like Superman!

It is the most fantastic feeling.

I spread out my front paws for balance, just like the ski jumpers. Then—*ooooff!*—an instant later I come down for a landing.

It isn't exactly a soft landing. But it is on target, right in the middle of the pillow. I lie still for a moment, my eyes closed, catching my breath.

"Marvin! Are you all right?"

I open my eyes to see Raymond and Fats hovering over me.

"I think so," I reply.

I check all my moving parts. They still appear to be moving. As I get slowly to my feet, I can tell that my bones are intact. And my valuable brain is undamaged.

"You did it!" Fats is bouncing with excitement.

"My pillow calculations proved to be correct." Raymond looks pleased with himself.

"Yes," I say. "Once again I have done what no mouse has ever done before. First, I broke the world speed record for land travel by a mouse. And now I have become the world's first ski-jumping mouse."

"Hip, hip, hooray!" cheers Fats.

"From now on," I decide, "you can call me by my new name."

"What's that?" asks Fats.

"Merciless Marvin the Magnificent," I say, "the Flying Mouse."

After my big triumph, it really is time to pack up and move back to Macy's.

"Gang," I say the next morning. "We leave today."

Fats is a little reluctant to leave the scene of all his glory. Not to mention the convenience of living right inside a restaurant.

"So soon?" he says.

But I remind him of our cozy little dollhouse with the convenience of its own kitchen. Not to mention the toy department with all its games to play, the furniture department with its beds to bounce on, the TV department, and the gourmet shop just an escalator ride away.

"The gourmet shop doesn't have coconut donuts," he reminds me.

"True," I reply. "But the toy department has finger paints."

"Really?"

I nod.

Fats's face lights up.

"Oh, wow! I never tried finger paints."

And just like that, he is ready to go.

Raymond selects a few of his most precious found objects, ties them up in his baby sock, and he is ready too.

We stop for a moment at Fats's little gallery to take a last look at his one-mouse show.

"Exciting!" says Fats.

"Provocative!" says Raymond.

"Unique!" I say. "Whoever that mystery artist is, he is extremely talented."

And then we take our place under the counter nearest the museum's front door. We watch the hands of the clock as they slowly move toward opening time. The workers arrive. The guard takes his place at the door.

At exactly nine o'clock, the guard opens the door.

"Good-bye, Googlestein Museum," I mutter under my breath.

"Guggenheim," corrects Raymond.

People come streaming in. And we go out.